THE LEVEE

THE LEVEE

A NOVEL OF BATON ROUGE

Malcolm Shuman

ACADEMY

CHICAGO

FOR SHAWN, WITH AFFECTION AND RESPECT

Academy Chicago Publishers
363 West Erie Street
Chicago, Illinois 60654

First published in 2008. Reprinted in 2009.

© 2008 Malcolm K. Shuman

Printed and bound in the U.S.A.

Library of Congress Cataloging-in-Publication Data on file with the publisher

CHAPTER ONE

When I was fifteen we used to drive down to the levee to camp. We would go on Saturdays, as soon as the weather got warm, and we would build a fire, set up a tent, and twist biscuit dough around sticks and cook beans. There was Stan Chandler, who was my best friend, and Toby Hobbs, who was nobody's best friend, but was the only one of us who, at fifteen, had a car, and sometimes there was Blaize St. Martin, who was skinny and asthmatic, and whose mother was afraid for his health, so that he often had to sneak away.

The place where we camped was five miles south of the city, across the levee from an abandoned plantation called Windsong. We would sit cross-legged on the grassy top of the levee at dusk and stare across the gravel river road at the hulk of the big house, with the slave cabins behind it in the distance and tell stories about Civil War battles and slave revolts and the ghosts who were reputed to still walk the fields at night. When it grew dark we would turn on our flashlights and make our way down the other side of the dike to the borrow pit. If it was spring or early summer, we would launch Stan's aluminum canoe to cross the fifty feet of murky water. If it was late in the summer or in the early fall, we would walk across the dry surface of the pit until we reached the high ground on the other side. Then, near the tent we'd pitched in a clearing hacked free of blackberry vines and grasses, we would build a fire.

1

It was a time before cell phones, and nearly all televisions were black and white. We would sit beside the leaping flames, even on the warmest nights, and look upstream at the lights of the city, as we breathed in the hot, rich smell of the river that stretched for a mile in front of us all the way to the thin line of willows on the other side. We would bring frozen biscuits to bake in the fire, and frozen pot pies and sometimes beans. I had a bolt action .22 Marlin rifle, which my poet-father had purchased for me because a rifle was what a man gave to his son. But other than the first time he had driven me to the levee with it, when I was ten, he'd never taken me to shoot it again. Toby brought his father's .32 Colt, spirited away from the desk drawer where it was kept. Toby's father was an assistant attorney general for the State of Louisiana and Toby bragged that his old man could fix any problems with the law.

Sometimes we shot snakes in the borrow pit and sometimes just tin cans at the base of the levee and once I shot at crows, flying high over the river and when I saw one drop out of formation, wounded, I felt ashamed.

But mostly we sat around the fire and told stories.

Since we were fifteen years old we talked about girls a lot because in that day we were all virgins, though Toby would have had us believe otherwise. He told us of the girls he'd had (no one believed him, because he was red-haired, overweight and exuded insincerity) and of the women we'd glimpsed coming and going from his home when his mother was away, and that we *did* believe. He told us about the big parties at the Heidelberg Hotel, downtown, when the legislature was in session, and about the high-class whores who attended, and we wondered how he knew so much.

We also talked about religion. Toby, who liked to shock, declared there was no God and cited Nietzsche. I said the world could not have come into existence by accident and, though I was coming to doubt the tenets of my Catholic upbringing, I could not deny the necessity for a prime mover. And Stanley, too small for sports and therefore devoted to his books, declared that the question was unanswerable but that faith was necessary for man's survival.

And, finally, we talked about Rufus Sikes.

On Sikes we were in total agreement. He was the meanest white trash son-of-a-bitch who'd ever lived and if there was a God, Sikes had been put on earth to test men's faith.

Of course, all white trash were mean, but Sikes was special. He was the overseer of Windsong, and he lived in a tumbledown shack a quarter mile downriver from the place where we camped, with his wife and more children than anyone could count, and rumor had it he hated Negroes worse than Willy Rainach and his pin-heads in the legislature who'd just butted heads with crazy Governor Earl Long.

It was well known that some years back Sikes had knifed a man in front of Bergeron's Store, a country grocery on the River Road that was our source of provisions. He'd gotten a year for assault with a deadly weapon. After that, people steered clear of Sikes, which was easy because of where he lived: he seldom went into the city during the day time and subsisted on a house garden, some chickens and, rumor had it, whatever he could get by burglary. The black children who lived in the line of shotgun houses along the River Road kept off his property, but sometimes, at night, they rode past his house on their bikes and threw firecrackers in his yard.

He usually replied with his shotgun and it was, everyone thought, a miracle that nobody was killed.

The killings were all of grownups. Women, to be accurate.

That's what we talked about that May night.

I said I thought it was bullshit, that no one could kill a bunch of people in this day and age and not be caught.

Toby said not everything made the newspapers and that his father, who used to be an assistant D.A., had once had a cabinet full of unsolved murder cases. They were the ones where either the victims were too poor to merit much investigation, or the accused was rich enough to hire a high-priced lawyer, or where the victim was black.

"If it's a white man killed a nigger, they don't do anything, and if it's one nigger killed another one, nobody cares, either, unless they catch the nigger did it. Then they fry him." Toby grinned, an evil jack-o-lantern whose leer flickered in the flames of the campfire.

"My old man saw 'em electrocute a nigger once," he went on. "Said it smelled just like pork frying. White man smells different, more like beef."

I got up feeling sick and went to stand on the riverbank.

"Toby, you're full of shit," Stan said, turning the stick with the biscuit dough. "You told us Chinese women have sideways pussies."

"They do."

"Like I said, you're full of shit. I checked in one of my dad's medical books."

Toby roused himself. "I don't have to stay here and listen to that, shithead. I could've spent tonight getting some instead of hauling your ass to the levee. For all I know, you wanted to come here because you're queer like Blaize and want to give me and Colin a blow job."

"Blaize isn't queer," Stan said. "And you're a fat, lying asshole."

"Maybe I will go get some ass, then," Toby said. "You wanna come, Colin? Wanna leave fairy boy here by himself while we go punch a pussy?"

"I came to camp," I said.

"Then you're both fairies," Toby snorted. "Have fun together." He gave the round mouth, mimicking what we imagined a homosexual must look like giving fellatio.

"You're leaving?" Stan asked.

"Goddamn right. I got a woman waiting for me. Don't worry—I'll come back tomorrow morning to get you little girls."

"Don't take the fucking canoe," Stan told him.

"I don't need your goddamn canoe. I can get across the borrow pit. Only cunts need a canoe."

We watched him go, crashing through the high grass like an elephant.

"You think he's really got a woman?" I asked.

"He's a lying sack of shit." Stan turned the biscuits again. "He'll be back by midnight. If his fat ass doesn't fall into the water."

Minutes later the car started and then we heard it slip into gear. A few seconds later the engine sounds died away. We were alone.

"We're better off without him," Stan said. "He's gonna get us in trouble anyway."

"Yeah." I leaned back and watched him peel the cooked biscuits off the stick, burning his fingers and sticking them in his mouth.

"You think Sikes really killed a bunch of women?" I asked.

"You think my old man and yours would let us come down here if he had?" Stan asked. "That's just some of Toby's bullshit."

We ate the biscuits and our beans and a cinnamon twist that Stan had brought and drank water from our canteens and watched the shadows of the big ships gliding down the river in the darkness, their running lights red and green like Christmas ornaments. We talked about what it must be like to be the captain of an oil tanker, and how tricky the river was, and Stan said that once, a long time ago, when his father was a medical student, he and some others had swum it, up near St. Francisville. Then we looked up at the stars and talked about life in outer space and whether there might be some advanced race, with a Klatu and a giant robot, looking down at us, like in *The Day the Earth Stood Still*. And when it was midnight Toby still hadn't come back.

"So he decided to sleep at his own house," Stan said. "If he doesn't come back by morning we'll go down to Bergeron's and call my mom to come get us."

"Maybe something happened to him," I said.

"Like what?"

"I don't know. Maybe Sikes got him."

"Shit. What would Sikes want with *him*?"

"Maybe his car got stuck or broke down."

"Good. We don't need him. You're the one said he had a car, let's invite him. I knew his fat ass wouldn't stay out here all night."

"I'm serious, Stan. Maybe we ought to go up on the levee and look, just to make sure."

He sighed and finally gave a little shrug. "All right."

You can't take anything back. But if I could, I would take back that moment.

CHAPTER TWO

It is a hotel for gamblers, built to capitalize on the nearest of the two riverboats moored alongside the levee. There is something called Downtown Development, which is a way of trying to reverse white flight by throwing money at the downtown area and hoping enough people from the suburbs will come for festivals and other events, and that enough conventioneers will come from out of town to lose their money. At least, that's what the car rental agent said at the airport counter. He was a burly man in his late thirties, named Annunzio, and he asked if I was coming to a convention or to gamble and I told him neither. I asked if the names Hobbs, Chandler or St. Martin meant anything to him and he said no. Then I tried the name Sikes and he didn't know it, either. Finally, I tried Drood and he hesitated and then said it sounded like the name of a street in the southern part of town, which made sense.

It didn't matter because I checked them all out before I came here and the only one in the book is St. Martin. B. St. Martin, to be exact, but that could be Benjamin or Belle or Blanche. And I was too cowardly to call before I left.

So now, in the middle of a warm Sunday afternoon in May, I stand in the fresh-scented hotel room and stare out the north-facing window at the state capitol, with the river to the left, and wonder what I'm going to say when I pick up the phone.

"*Blaize, I remember some things from back then, the spring of 'fifty-nine. But I don't know if they're true. Maybe I invented them. More than anything, there's this black pit that keeps sucking me toward it, like a whirlpool in the river, and I know the truth is down there, but I may have to drown to find out what it is.*"

"*Aren't you a true crime writer? It's all public record. Old newspapers and things.*"

"*I'm also a coward. I can't make myself do the research. I thought maybe if I came back . . .*"

"*I'm not this Blaize. You must want somebody else.*"

And the phone would click.

I know I won't get off that easily.

Blaize is old family. They never move away.

Everything out there is different, which I expected, because, after all, it's been over thirty years since I was here to bury my father, and over forty since I actually was a resident. I had to use a road map to get here from the airport, on the new throughway, even though every Saturday, as a boy, I went downtown to the Louisiana Theater to watch the double feature western.

I asked about the old Red Sticks, the minor league baseball team, and I was told they built the throughway right over the stadium from which Big Roger McKee once hit a home run all the way to Dalrymple Drive, on the edge of the lake.

The Heidelberg Hotel, once the lair of Huey Long and his cronies, has been renovated and its name changed, the last of several attempts to resuscitate it, I was told. Now it is a gleaming white, just down the street from the new performing arts center where an old auto hotel once stood. Maybe the downtown really will survive.

But I wonder as I stand here if maybe the whole image through this window has been painted on, to deceive the unwary. What can one say about gambling boats that don't cruise or a World War II destroyer permanently fixed to its dock, or a jet fighter rooted to its stand like an oversized model? Maybe if I go down I will see things the way they really are, in the city I remember from 1959, with two ferry boats that shuttle back and forth to Port Allen every half hour, with a load of cars and pedestrians. I remember the smell of those ferries, part grease from the huge diesel engines, and part popcorn and cotton candy from the concession on the top deck. I remember looking down at the stern wheel, endlessly churning brown river water into a white froth, and I remember the huge, tireless eccentric arm that drove the engine, never stopping until the boat docked.

In those days, the only bridge was five miles upriver, near the refineries, and it wasn't built until 1941. When I lived here, everyone took the ferry.

Of course, I know the scene isn't painted on. It is real and what is unreal is my memory. Perhaps none of it happened at all.

I turn around to stare at the phone.

Maybe, I think, I should just drive out there, not give him a chance to hang up. Maybe as I drive past I'll see him in the yard, and stop "by accident." Or maybe if it isn't him, I can pretend to be lost, ask directions, and assure myself that the St. Martin I'm looking for never lived at this address. People work in their yards on Sunday afternoons. It seems like a plan.

I drive out through the university, under the canopy of oaks that cover Nicholson Drive, and between the two great cathedrals, Tiger Stadium for football, and Alex Box, where baseball is played. Once my father took me to a football game but I knew it bored him. He said that the university had misplaced its priorities, and being a faculty member, he resented the fact that the football coach made more than the professors. But we went to baseball games often. Even though the team was mediocre, he seemed to forget his resentment against sports as we sat on the hard bleachers in the afternoon sun, rooting for the home team. I wondered later if it was because baseball was no threat to him, but later I realized it was because it took him back to a time in his own youth before he knew he would be a poet and not an athlete. In watching the team play he saw himself the way it might have been. Happy days, before he met the love of his life, who died.

Once I leave the university I get lost, it has all changed that much. The address I'm looking for is out on Highland Road, but it is in a subdivision that was a cotton field when I was growing up. Now it is a stylish middle-class community with twenty-five-year-old houses and well-kept lawns. I circle down streets that resemble mobius loops and end up in cul-de-sacs more than once before I find the street where the map says it should be.

The house is one story, ranch-style, and there's no one working in the garden. I'm not even sure anyone is home, because there is no light visible through the crack in the curtain drawn over the picture window. I sit at the curb, engine running, and try to decide what the house tells me. No toys on the close-clipped front lawn, but, then, we are all old enough to be grandparents by now. A single gray Honda Minivan rests in the shade of the carport. The other slot is empty.

I can always go up to the door and knock.

But I am a coward. What will I do if he opens it?

I leave the subdivision and start back for the hotel.

Once I reach the university I make a left, heading for the River Road. But when I get to it, I hesitate. A right will take me downtown, where I started. And a left will take me away from town. To Windsong.

I am not ready yet.

The hotel room is my haven. I can stay here as long as I want, a god looking down on the people in the streets below. Some are walking along the levee, on a bicycle path, and a gaggle of teenagers lingers at the fountain. A charter bus has pulled up near the naval museum and I watch to see who gets out.

• • •

Carolyn said I should come, would have come with me, except that she still has school and they don't let high school teachers just fly off for a week. I promised I'd call every night.

Now, as the afternoon light melts into evening gold and the sun starts to burn in obliquely through the tinted, north-facing window, I look back at the phone. Is she home right now, waiting for the call? Will I tell her I didn't have the courage to follow through after flying a thousand miles?

So I lift the phone and force myself to punch in the number. Not ours, but his. *B. St. Martin.*

I know it's Blaize before he says hello, because in that split instant between the time he picks up the receiver and the time he speaks I hear piano music in the background.

"This is Colin Douglas," I say finally. "Blaize?"

"Yes." His voice is deeper than I remember. "Colin?"

"Yeah, me. How are you?"

"I'm fine, Colin. Where are you?"

"Downtown, at the Sheraton. I was thinking about old times and I saw your name in the book."

"Old times," he says hesitantly. "Colin, did you come here to write a book?"

Now I understand the reserve.

"No," I say and imagine I can hear him exhale relief.

"I read a couple of your books," he says. "They made that TV movie out of one of them, didn't they?"

"Yeah. *Red Widow.*"

"That's right. I watched most of it. Pretty good."

"I didn't write the screenplay, if that makes a difference."

"I wondered." An awkward silence while the music, a Beethoven piano sonata, plays on in the background. "I always figured you'd come here and write about what happened."

"Once I thought I might. But I kept finding other projects."

"You have a project now?"

"Just a personal one." I tell him about the dreams. "I know the basics but I can't be sure if all I remember's accurate. Sometimes I seem to remember different things in the dreams, like it happened some other way."

"It was a long time ago, Colin. I try not to think about it."

It sounds like a judgment.

"Do you know where any of the others are?" I ask. "Toby or Stan?"

"No. I think Toby got into some trouble a few years ago. He was into real estate. I haven't heard anything about Stan for forty years. To tell the truth, I haven't tried to find out, and I don't go to class reunions."

"You still play the piano?" I ask.

"Not as much," he says. "But I like to listen."

"So how's life?" I try again, desperate to prolong the conversation. "You have children? Grandkids?"

"A son," he says. "He's thirty-two, divorced. Lives in Houston, near his mother."

"Oh." The music finishes. "Look, maybe we could meet for lunch tomorrow."

"I'd like to, Colin, but it's hard during the week. I teach, you know. One of the public high schools. It's pretty much an all-day business."

It's a polite way of saying no and I can only accept his decision. I tell him goodbye and disconnect.

Why should I be surprised that he's not glad to hear from me? What am I but a specter carrying my own contagion?

• • •

That night I walk down to the levee and look at the lights reflected in the water from the new bridge. A thread of music echoes from the *Belle*, the nearest gambling boat, and a languid breeze stirs the warm air. I find a hole-in-the-wall restaurant that serves po' boys and I have one with oysters, drowning the sandwich with a couple of draft beers.

When I get back my phone is ringing. I lift the receiver and hear Carolyn's voice.

"I just wanted to check," she says.

"Everything's fine." *God, I love this woman.*

"Have you talked to anybody?"

"Just Blaize. I don't think he wants to get back into it. Can't say I blame him."

"What will you do?"

"I don't know. Work up my courage and drive out there if I have to."

"Are you going to be all right?"

"Sure."

"Col and Honey say to tell you hi." The two grown kids, one in Boulder, the other in Los Angeles.

"What did you tell them?"

"Just that you were going home to do some research for something you were writing."

"I guess that's close enough."

"Colin . . ." There's fear in her voice, but all she says is: "I love you."

"I love you, too."

When we hang up I lie on the bed, wondering if I'll be able to sleep. I've read about sleepwalkers who rise from their dreams to act out problems that bother them during the day. Will I be found tomorrow wandering down the River Road in my skivvies?

But I am too tired to resist. I turn out the light and I dream.

CHAPTER THREE

We stood in the dark at the top of the levee, looking down. The air smelled of fresh grass and cow manure. Overhead, the moon rushed through stringy clouds. At the bottom of the slope, near the fence, a herd of cattle lay in a circle, a couple of them raising their heads as they sensed our presence.

"See?" Stan said. "He isn't here."

I glanced down at the gravel road, barely discernable in the night. To the left, a quarter-mile away, toward town, was the boxy outline of Bergeron's store, with no lights showing. The Bergerons had long since gone to bed. To the right, at the end of an oak avenue that began at the River Road, was the inky form of Windsong's big house, now a decaying ruin. And to the side of the entrance, strategically placed to guard the property, was the cabin of Rufus Sikes. It was dark, too.

There were no lights at all, until I saw something half a mile away, in the center of one of the fields. At first I thought it was my eyes playing tricks and I nudged Stan.

"Do you see something over there?"

"Where?"

I pointed. The light seemed to blink and then waver.

"I see it now," he said. "But why is somebody in the middle of the field at this time of night?"

"It's the old graveyard," I said.

There was a cemetery on Windsong, where several generations of black laborers were buried. I'd never been there, but I'd had the place pointed out to me when we'd been riding down the River Road looking for a place to shoot tin cans. It was at the end of a dirt road, a quarter of a mile back in the fields, and cloaked by cedars.

"Jesus, Colin, you're right. But why?"

"What if it's Toby? What if he's in trouble?"

"What the hell would he be doing in a graveyard?"

"I dunno. Why would *anybody* be poking around down there at midnight?"

We stood silently for a moment.

"Look, I say we go down and check it," I said.

Stan hesitated. "Maybe it's something that's none of our business."

"Like what?"

"Like maybe it's just some guy knocking off a piece. What we gonna do, go up and shine a light in his eyes?"

"That's a flashlight," I said. "You think they're outside screwing on the grass? People screw in cars."

"I still don't think it's Toby."

"We'll never know if we stand here with our thumbs up our asses. And if it turns out it really was Toby and we didn't do shit, you wanna live with that?"

"What the hell would we do if it was? Make a noise like a siren?"

"We got my .22."

"That's what I figured you'd say," he said miserably.

I started forward and a second later he followed.

"Okay, hold up, I'm coming."

Later I wondered what would have happened if I'd listened to Stan and not gone.

It took us twenty minutes of walking along the levee top to get to the place where the little trail led off the main road. In that time the dancing light had vanished and a couple of times Stan lagged, suggesting we turn back, but I'd refused. Now we stood looking down at the rutted track.

"I don't see anything," he said. "Let's go."

The moon ducked under a cloud and the fields lapsed into darkness.

"Look." I halted. There was movement below and as we watched, a light-colored car with its headlamps off bounced over the ruts and swung onto the gravel in a spray of dust that rose up like a fog, obscuring vehicle and driver. By the time the dust lifted, the car was barely visible, headed in the direction of town.

"Did you get a look?" I asked Stan.

He shook his head. "It may have been a Ford. Or a Chevy. He was in a hurry, whoever it was."

I started down, toward the road.

"Where you going?" he called after me.

"He was running from something."

"Maybe he saw us."

"Nah. He took off from the cemetery. He wouldn't have seen us from there."

"You think it was Toby?"

"Why would he be taking off like that?"

Stan hesitated. "Let's go back."

"No. I want to see why he was leaving in such a hurry."

"But that's the graveyard."

"You scared of ghosts?"

"Shit, no. But maybe it's something else."

"Like what?"

He shrugged in the darkness.

I reached the fence and motioned for him to separate the top and middle strands while I ducked under.

"You're really going to the cemetery?" he asked.

"Hell yes. Look, why don't you stay up here with the rifle and cover me. If the boogie man comes chasing after me, you can knock him off from the top of the levee. How's that?"

"You don't want me to come?"

"I want you to stay right here, okay? I'll be fine."

"You think you're Paladin," he accused.

"No, I'm the fucking Lone Ranger and you're Tonto."

"Fuck you. Tonto means stupid, Señorita Gloria says."

"Like I said . . ."

"Asshole."

"Just cover me."

I hurried across the road, my steps exploding like gunshots on the gravel. When I got to the cemetery track on the other side I stopped, listening.

But there were no sounds except for a far-away boat horn on the river.

The way ahead was a black tunnel, between straggly trees that lined the sides of the little trail. A quarter of a mile. Two city blocks. No sweat.

Paladin had a hand-crafted revolver, though, and a hideout Derringer. I had a flashlight and a friend who was scared of his shadow.

I walked forward, wondering if I was being stupid; Stan couldn't see me after a certain point. I turned to look back at the levee, to see if I could make him out at the top, silhouetted against the sky, but I couldn't be sure.

What if there really was something at the end of this road—something that was watching even as I walked?

The trees on each side seemed to lean toward me, narrowing the tunnel as I went. I thought about turning on the flashlight but decided against it: if there really was somebody—or *something*—at the cemetery it would be able to see me long before I knew it was watching.

Suddenly a hand grabbed my ankle and I gave a little yell. Then, as I flipped on the light, I realized I'd tripped in a rut.

So much for surprise.

I switched off the light, moved to the side of the trail, and waited.

Silence.

It was crazy to be scared. There weren't any werewolves or vampires or bogeymen. Only characters like Rufus Sikes, and there was no reason for him to be down here at this time of night.

Was there?

Screw Sikes. I was almost there. A few more yards and I'd be to the graves and I'd shine my light around, probably see a discarded Trojan from the guy in the car, and then I'd walk back and tell Stan what a pussy he was.

For some reason my heart was beating loud enough to shake my body.

I sucked in a couple of deep breaths. I could see it ahead now, the cemetery with its pale white stones. Nothing unusual, nothing out of the ordinary.

And then I heard it.

At first I thought it was a dog howling far away but then I realized it was a moan.

I froze.

It was coming from the graveyard.

Oh Christ.

And suddenly it was rising up in front of me, a white form congealing out of the stones, wavering like ectoplasm against the darkness, long, liquid hair, skull-white face, hands beckoning like talons.

I ran and didn't stop until I could see the levee. I looked over my shoulder, half afraid it was coming after me, but there was nothing.

"Stan?" No answer. "Stan, goddamnit, where are you?" Nothing.

Jesus, had something gotten him while I was down there? Terror started to shake me like a rag doll. What if I was alone? What if he'd been plucked away and I was to be next?

I slipped under the barbed wire, tearing my shirt on the top strand, and ran up the side of the grassy slope to the top of the levee.

"Stan!"

He was crumpled in a heap just on the river side, his head on his arm, and the rifle across his legs. I began to relax when I saw that his breathing was slow and regular.

"Stan."

His eyes opened and he sat up.

"I guess I fell asleep."

"I guess you did, asshole."

"Did you see anything?"

"I . . ." Sure, a ghost. That would make me the laughingstock of everybody at school.

"No," I said. "I didn't see anything at all."

CHAPTER FOUR

I awaken drenched in sweat, shouting into the darkness. But I am not lying on the grass. I am on clean sheets, in a scented room. Alone.

But where? For a second my mind churns. Is there a television interview this morning? Is this Milwaukee or St. Louis? What book will I be asked about today? I replay over and over the dreams that started it all, dreams of interviewers leaning toward me with dripping fangs, asking me about THE BOOK, except that it wasn't any of the books I'd written, but the one that's stayed anchored in my mind over the years. The one I'm afraid to write. And they ask me, these vampire interviewers, what it is I really saw that night.

And I cannot tell them because I don't know.

The last TV interview was a dismal failure and my editor, alarmed, called me afterwards to ask what happened. It was a book about a woman who had methodically poisoned four husbands and finally been convicted, thanks to the persistence of the last victim's son. The book was called *Red Widow*, because of her favorite clothing color. And in the middle of the interview, which fortunately was with a station in Albuquerque and not Los Angeles or Houston or New Orleans, I'd choked. There were people who'd been on the levee that night, I'd blurted, who should have seen.

The interviewer, a black-haired, attractive young woman named Inez, blinked, because there was no levee in the book, but since interviewers seldom read the books anyway, she figured it was something that wasn't in the blurb she'd skimmed before air time, and she asked if I'd talked to any of them, and I only looked blank.

Time ran out before things could get any worse, but a bookstore owner called my editor, and I got a call that evening in the hotel.

"Is everything okay?" she asked.

"Just tired," I mumbled. "This makes ten cities in ten days. I get confused."

"There're two more cities on the tour. Can you handle it?"

"Yeah, Myra, sure."

"Colin, you sound tired. I think you need a rest."

"I'm fine."

I must have snapped at her because the next morning, before leaving for the airport, I got a call from my agent, a tall, tweedy man who got out of editing when he realized he could make more money representing writers than publishing them.

"They're concerned," Gordon Gayle said in his cultured Boston voice. "Maybe you've been working too hard. Maybe we ought to cancel on the last two cities."

"I can manage."

"Look, Colin, if it's too much of a strain it isn't worth it. Is there something we need to talk about? Something that's bothering you?"

"I'm fine, Gordon. How many times do I have to say it? F-I-N-E."

"Then why did you refuse Baton Rouge as a tour stop? This was supposed to be your big chance, but you wouldn't go to your own home town."

"That's personal."

"Colin, nothing's personal if it's going to give you a nervous breakdown. Look, I talked to Carolyn before I called you."

"Damn it, Gordon, you had no right."

"She says you've had some problems lately. She's concerned, as are we all."

I suddenly felt naked, betrayed. Would Carolyn really have told him about the dreams, the long walks at night, the blank stares as if I'd gone into another dimension?

And, of course, because she loved me, she would have.

All the energy suddenly leaked out of me. "What do you want me to do, Gordon?"

"I want you to talk things over with someone. Get some of the heat off. Nothing long-term. Writing's a gut-wrenching process. You open a vein and bleed and if you're lucky a publisher wants your blood type. But there's no security. Look, Colin, you're one of the saner writers I handle. So humor me and let's take care of this, nip it in the bud, and then you can get back to work, ay?"

So I saw a psychologist, and he asked me about my parents (mother dead in 1952 of a brain hemorrhage, father dead of a heart attack in 1970, at the age of 53). The psychologist made a big thing over the fact that I'd outlived both my parents and was an only child. Then I told him about the execution and he began to write fast on the pad.

The condemned man was named Delmos Bridges and he'd been convicted of murdering two little boys.

The first boy had been taken from a playground in Austin, Texas, the second, months later, from a summer day camp in the same city. There had been no clues until one of the counselors at the day camp remembered a white van parked by the curb. The bodies of both boys were later found in woods a few miles from where they'd been abducted.

A year later, in Norman, Oklahoma, a man in a white van tried to kidnap another boy from a bus stop, but onlookers rushed to the child's aid and one of them got a partial plate number. The number led to an unemployed house painter named Delmos Bridges.

At first he denied everything, but physical evidence soon linked him to the two murders. Faced with the DNA and fibers from his van on the victims' bodies, Delmos Bridges confessed his crimes, but alluded to others that would never be solved without his help.

Convicted in Texas and sentenced to death, for the next two years he led lawmen on a six-state goose chase that promised much and delivered disappointingly little. There were other victims, he swore, but when the burial places were searched, no bodies turned up. Sometimes there were missing children in those areas who fit the descriptions of the children he claimed to have killed, but without bodies there was little to be done. In the one instance where a body was found, it was of an older woman, not a ten-year-old boy. She had been hit on the head by a heavy object, while he claimed that he had strangled the boy. Faced with the disparities, he revised his story, claiming he'd kidnapped both mother and child and that the boy had yet to be found.

It became clear that Delmos Bridges was a cunning liar who had committed many crimes but told the truth about few of them, and that he was enjoying making fools of the police.

I'd read the newspaper accounts with only ordinary interest. It was only after his letter landed in my mailbox that the possibility of writing about his crimes occurred to me.

Dear Mr. Douglas:

I have read your book the MAN KILLER about the man who killed all those women & being somebody with experence in that aria I thought Id write & see if you want to talk to me about writing my life too. I have a lot more exper-

ence killing then he does & I can tell you things you probably dont know about how it feels. You can write me at the above address in Huntsville, but you better hurry because they aim to put a needle in my arm before too many more apeels. Looking forward to hering from you,
   Sincerly,
   Delmos Bridges

At first I thought it was a bad joke, but then I realized the postmark was real. I showed the letter to Carolyn, as one of those curiosities that pops up with some frequency in the life of someone in my profession, and I assured her that I had no intention of replying.

I'd just refresh my memory of Bridges' crimes by scanning some of the news accounts from 1996, the year the first murder had occurred.

And then I'd read about his trial and the search for more victims.

And when Gordon Gayle asked me what I planned to write next I told him I had an idea.

Carolyn was horrified.

I'd told her about the levee and what had happened nearly fifty years ago, how some of us had been caught up in something we couldn't understand at the time, and how I guessed it was part of the reason I did what I did now, trying to see how other people reacted in similar situations. But there were things about the levee I'd never told her or anyone else, and up to now they'd stayed buried. When I explained about going to see Delmos Bridges she immediately sensed that it might start a process that couldn't be stopped.

I told her she was an alarmist, that this was a once-in-a-lifetime chance. He could have written to Ann Rule or a host of other true crime writers, but he'd chosen me. Up to now, I'd

written books based on what policemen said, what the families of victims said, what coroners and reporters and judges and
lawyers said. I'd observed the accused at pretrial hearings, at
trial, and during appeals. But never before had I had the chance
to sit down across from a confessed serial killer and hear him
tell me in his own words what he'd done.

"You don't think this is just the kind of attention he wants?"
she asked.

"It may be. But this is what I do, hon. And he isn't talking
to anybody else, not the FBI profilers, not the Rangers or anybody. He led them all over six states with a bunch of lies and
when they gave up, he shut up. But whatever he is, he has a past,
a childhood, parents, maybe brothers and sisters. If I can get
through his ego to whatever makes him the way he is, maybe
that will help keep somebody else from turning out that way."

"And that's why you're doing it?" she asked.

I shrugged, unable to look her in the eye. "One reason," I
said.

• • •

My relationship with Delmos Bridges lasted two years. It
started tentatively, with a trip to Death Row, then became a
series of monthly visits.

He seemed to look forward to my coming, but I dreaded every
minute.

The bastard enjoyed telling what he'd done, as if he were reliv-
ing every delicious moment. And he could see my revulsion,
because he would leer with ragged yellow teeth, and cackle. He
knew no matter how much he disgusted me I was hooked.

And every once in a while he'd slip in a question about myself.
What was my wife like? Did I have children? Grandchildren?

He'd back off when my jaw set, give a little shrug as if to say I was overreacting, draw on his cigarette, and then say, "Where were we?"

Every time I came home to Colorado, Carolyn noticed the change.

For one thing, she said, I seemed to take longer in the shower, as if I needed more time to wash myself clean. For another, our sex life began to falter: When I should have been thinking about her, I would see his leering face.

"Do you *have* to write it?" she asked one night as we lay together in the upstairs bedroom of the old house we'd bought thirty years before and fixed up, the house where our kids had been reared.

"I've signed an agreement with him. He's giving his share of the royalties to an abused children's fund. I think that's his sick joke. But maybe it will help some kids."

"And when the time comes?"

I exhaled. "He wants me there."

She frowned. "How can you?"

"I'll have to force myself. But I've come this far. I can't just back out because I'm squeamish."

She turned toward me then in the big bed, put her hands with their long fingers along my face and looked into my eyes.

"My poor Colin, what's this doing to you? This isn't about him, is it?"

"I don't know," I said truthfully.

Two months later I was seated opposite him for the last time and he asked the same question a psychologist would ask weeks later: "Why do you think you write about murders, Mr. Douglas?"

He smiled his ragged, yellow-toothed smile and I didn't have an answer. And four hours later, while I watched him die, the only person he had invited, I still didn't know. And I started to dream about the levee.

I started to dream about that night, walking along the grassy top with Stan, heading for the old cemetery with the flickering light, and I dreamed about walking by myself down the dirt track toward the leaning gravestones. And I dreamed about the moans and about what I saw, wavering ahead of me in the night.

But when I'd awaken I could never remember what it was. A form, a face, a person?

Intellectually, of course, I knew what it had to be, because I knew what had happened afterwards, but the more I had the dreams, the more I began to wonder if I'd ever walked down that lonely stretch at all. Had Stanley and I ever left the campsite or had we both gone to sleep and waked up the next morning to find our world forever changed? Had I only invented what might have happened, let my guilt thrust me into an imaginary situation where I became an actor instead of an observer? If so, why?

There was no one left to tell me the truth. Stan was long gone, and Toby and Blaize hadn't been there. But if I'd said something to one of them in the days immediately afterward, maybe if I could talk to one of them, it would reveal whether my memory was truthful or trying to drive me insane. And maybe if I went back, stood where my memory told me I'd been—maybe then it would all shake loose.

And so I am back, grabbing at the shreds of the white, fleeting ghost as it melts back into memory, and I am once more afraid.

CHAPTER FIVE

I awoke in the grayness of dawn, staring up at top of the tent. I struggled out of my sleeping bag and pulled on my jeans, sooty-smelling from the campfire. Stan still slept in his own bag, beside me. I shivered in the cold mist, found matches and some tinder and started a fire.

In the gray, enveloping fog the only signs of the river were the sloshing of water against its banks and the smell of mud.

I untied the provisions from where they dangled in a paper bag from the limb of a gum tree and put bacon into the skillet. When it was done, I cracked four eggs, scrambled them with the camp spoon, and was just taking the skillet off the fire when Stan emerged from the tent, rubbing his eyes.

"Did Toby come back?" he asked.

"Do you see him?"

"That bastard." He stumbled over to the edge of the clearing and relieved himself. When he was finished he ambled back to the campfire and reached for a plate.

"You want me to make some coffee?" he asked.

"That would be good."

He poured water from his canteen into an aluminum pot and then stuck the pot into the flames.

"Colin, about last night . . ."

"Yeah?"

"What do you reckon that light was down there?"

I shrugged. "Beats the shit out of me."

We ate, drank hot black coffee that tasted of wood smoke, and said no more about the strange events of the night before.

When we'd finished eating and scrubbed the pots and pans, Stan went to sit on the river bank, his legs hanging over. Below, lazy waves slopped against the mud verge, and as the fog lifted we could see logs and other flotsam bobbing and turning in the current on the way to the Gulf.

"You ever think about what it's like to be dead," he said suddenly.

"What?"

"To be dead. Not to exist."

"Yeah, I've thought about it. But there's got to be something afterwards."

"You mean like there has to be something afterwards for those logs out there after they fall in the river?"

"We ain't logs, for Christ's sake."

"You sure?"

"I'm sure I'm not a fucking log. What's got you thinking about this kind of crap?"

He didn't answer. "Maybe none of this is real. Maybe if I swam out in the river and drowned, I'd wake up in bed, somewhere else."

"Maybe if frogs had wings they wouldn't bump their asses on the ground."

"I'm serious, Colin."

"You want to wake up somewhere else?"

"Sometimes."

"Why, for fuck's sake?"

He didn't answer, just stared moodily out at the brown river.

I never knew if it was the dirt overhang giving way under his weight or whether he lurched forward intentionally but I saw the movement, heard the crack as the dirt began to thunder downward. I reached out reflexively and caught him as earth crashed into the water ten feet below and he thrashed in my grip.

"Jesus, hold on," I panted, reaching out my other hand. He grabbed it and I slowly dragged him up the bluff and onto the bank. For a second he didn't speak and then he heaved a sigh.

"I guess it gave out from under me."

"I guess so."

He got up and brushed himself off, but I was still shaking.

"You fall in the river, I'm not going after you," I warned. "That current's going twenty miles an hour. They won't find your ass 'til you get to Cuba."

"Don't worry." He slapped a last chunk of mud off his jeans. "You ready to take down the tent?"

We struck camp, stuffing the tent back into its canvas pouch, and dousing the fire. He didn't say more than the bare minimum as we carried the equipment down to the canoe and then shoved off across the placid borrow pit. A water snake, usually fair game for the rifle, uncoiled itself from a nearby branch, but Stan ignored it. When we reached the levee he jumped out, pulled the canoe onto dry land, and held it while I clambered out.

I looked up at the top of the dike, hoping to see Toby's car, but instead what I saw was a white sheriff's cruiser, making its way slowly along the levee top in the direction of town.

I got a sinking feeling. We weren't breaking any laws, but you never knew what new rule they'd come up with. The cruiser slowed and came to a stop as the deputy sighted us.

"Shit," I said under my breath.

"You boys want to come up here?" the deputy called down, opening his door.

Stan laid the rifle against the side of the canoe and we headed up the levee.

The deputy was a paunchy man with a ruddy face, white hair and sky-blue eyes, and I wondered if Toby's old man had the pull to handle him if we'd committed some obscure infraction.

"You find anything to shoot with that rifle?" the man asked.

"Snakes and tin cans," I said. The deputy nodded.

"You boys been out here all night?"

I nodded. "Yes, sir."

"Just you two?"

Stan and I exchanged glances. "Toby left last night," I said. "He didn't want to stay. Toby Hobbs."

I waited to see if the name would mean anything but nothing registered in the deputy's face.

"Y'all come out here very much?"

"Sometimes on weekends."

He stared at us as if the silence might make us crack open but we didn't offer anything else.

"You got names?" he asked then. We told him.

"We breaking some kind of law?" I asked.

He didn't answer. "Your folks know where you are?"

"Yes, sir."

"What did you do last night?"

"What do you mean?" Stan asked.

"I mean did you stay over by the river or did you come over to the levee side, maybe do a little exploring?"

Stan looked at me. I decided it wasn't a good time to lie.

"About midnight we wondered where Toby was and we came back over to this side and walked down the levee to see if we saw his car."

"About midnight, you say?"

"More or less."

"And did you see any cars?"

I hesitated. "Only car we saw was one coming from the cemetery down there."

The deputy was staring at us now.

"What kind of car?"

"I don't know. We were on top of the levee and there was a lot of dust. It was white."

"Or light brown," Stan put in.

"It was white," I insisted.

The deputy looked from one of us to the other. "Either of you see the driver or how many people was in it?"

"No, sir," we both said, shaking our heads.

"Which way was it heading?"

"Toward town," I said. "It had its lights off. At least, 'til it got about to Bergeron's."

"You didn't see nothing else?"

I didn't say anything but then Stan blurted out, "There was a light."

"A light?"

"Out by the cemetery. Like a flashlight or something." It was clear now that the deputy wasn't interested in us except as witnesses, so I gathered up my courage.

"What's this about, Mister? What happened?"

The deputy heaved a sigh. "Down by the cemetery last night— Somebody got killed."

My blood turned to ice.

"Who?" I finally managed.

"Dunno yet. They found her about a half hour ago."

"Her?" Stan said.

The deputy nodded. "A woman."

"Jeez," Stan said.

The deputy wrote down our names and addresses. "You got somebody coming for you?"

"I reckon," Stan said.

"Maybe I better give you a ride home."

"What about my canoe?" Stan asked.

"You can come back and get it later. Won't nobody steal it."

He helped us haul our gear up the hill to his car and took my rifle, removing the box magazine and then handing it to me. He loaded the gear into his trunk and as he called in on his radio I looked down the levee toward the cemetery. There were a couple of white cars parked on the River Road, but that was all I could make out.

As we made our way back to the city, I tried to think what my dad would say. We hadn't done anything, but you never could tell about parents.

It was Sunday morning, warm and quiet, with only a few cars out. Stan gave directions to his house in College Town, a university community just south of the campus gates.

The Chandlers lived in a two-story Spanish style home with a tile roof, spacious lawn, and a swimming pool in the back. The cream-colored Olds wasn't in the driveway so I figured Stan's father wasn't home. But his mother was—the cruiser had barely come to a halt before Mrs. Chandler shot out the front door, her thin face stricken.

"What's happened? Is something wrong?" she cried. The deputy unlimbered himself and shook his head:

"Everything's fine, ma'am. You this boy's mother?"

Mrs. C watched Stanley get out of the squad car. "Stanley. Did you do something? Is somebody hurt?"

"No, ma'am," the officer said. "Nobody's in trouble. Your husband around?"

"No. He's at a medical conference in Atlanta. Why?"

"Just thought maybe I should talk to him, too. But that's okay. The boys aren't in trouble. It's just there was a dead body found down on the River Road this morning and I thought your husband might want to go pick up the canoe. I didn't have a way to carry it back."

"A dead body?" Her hand flew to her throat. "Oh, my God. Who?"

"I don't know, ma'am. We're investigating now. But you may want to keep your boy away from the levee until we clear it up."

"Yes, of course." She grabbed Stanley then and crushed him against her. "Oh, my lord."

The deputy opened the trunk and helped lug Stan's gear up the walk to the front door. He and Stan's mother talked a little longer, but I couldn't hear what they were saying. Then the deputy patted Stan on the back and ambled back to the car.

"Dr. Chandler," he said. "My wife went to him once. Good doctor. Where does your dad work, son?"

"The university," I said. "English Department."

"He's a professor?"

"Yes, sir. A poet."

"A poet," he mused. "Well, I never was any good at poetry. You like poetry, do you?"

"Some of it."

"Yeah." He grinned. "Well, let's go see your folks."

"Just my dad," I said. "My mom's dead."

"I'm sorry. Look, I feel like a chauffeur with you back there and everybody sees us will think I'm taking you to jail. You want to ride up front with me?"

"Yes, sir."

"Good."

We headed past the lakes to Roseland Terrace, which would later become known as the Garden District, a tranquil area shaded by camphor trees and oaks. The district had been formed in the twenties when the university had been built on old Gartness Plantation, south of town, and a mix of university people, lawyers and state workers built the California-style bungalows, fake-Tudor cottages, and occasional Victorian monstrosities. Our own house, which my parents had bought right after the war, was a bungalow type with brick pillars holding up the screened front porch and a swing that rocked slowly in the breeze on rusty chains.

We stopped in the driveway, right behind the pale blue fifty-two Dodge my father had bought soon after my mother died. I got out, hoping to make it to the door first, but the deputy, with longer legs, beat me and was already pressing the doorbell.

I heard the chimes sound inside.

My father opened the door. He was in his shirtsleeves, not yet dressed for Mass, and for an instant he stared at the deputy as if the policeman might be from outer space.

The deputy, whose name I found out was Legier, explained while my father listened without expression. When the lawman had finished, my father turned to me.

"That true, you and Stanley were out looking for Toby?"

"Yes, sir."

"And you didn't see anything else?"

I thought of the white form, rising up toward me, and then I shook my head.

"No, sir."

"All right, take your gear and go on inside."

My father stayed talking to Legier for a few minutes more and then I heard the front door close and my father walked back to the breakfast room where I sat at the old green table where we ate our meals.

"I never liked you going out with Toby," my father said. "I never trusted him." He shook his head. "Leaving you and Stanley up there. Well, that won't happen again."

"Dad, did he say anything about the woman?"

My father blinked, a tall, thoughtful man who seemed to take an extra few seconds to register spoken words, as if he were turning all the possibilities over in his mind.

"No, son, he didn't say anything. Except that she was young, white, in her twenties."

"Did he say how?"

"Well, I think he said she'd been stabbed. Look, this isn't a good thing to talk about. Though I suppose it's natural to wonder, your being so close to it." He shook his head. "My God, do you know how close you came?" He reached out and hugged me to him. It was the first time I'd seen real emotion since my mother had died.

"I'm okay, Dad, really."

"Well, better get dressed. I think we have something to offer thanks for at Mass this morning."

It was only later that I got the news. It was just before supper and I was going over my history notes at the kitchen table where I studied when the phone rang and I heard my father let out a little gasp of surprise.

"Oh, my God. Are they sure?"

I froze, putting my notebook down on the table.

"No, the boys didn't see anything. I talked to the police. Right. Yes, you don't know how relieved I am. Well, thanks for calling. Yes. Of course. Did she have family here? I see. I'm sure they'll have something in the paper."

He hung up and I felt my hand start to tremble. When my father appeared in the doorway he was pale.

"That was Dr. O'Brien, my chairman," he said, his voice scarcely above a whisper. "They've identified the body on the River Road."

I felt my breath catch, waiting for the bullet to strike. My father shook his head, still disbelieving.

"I thought it would just turn out to be some woman from north Baton Rouge, you know, the kind who . . ." His voice trailed off.

He licked his lips. "Colin, it was Gloria Santana. The Spanish teacher at your school."

CHAPTER SIX

The phone rang several more times before I went to bed, but each time my father swooped on it. I could tell from his hushed voice, however, what he was discussing.

Stan's mother, I thought. She has to have spread the word and now people are calling to ask if it's true, whether we'd been out there, what, if anything, we'd seen.

I lay awake most of the night, wishing I could communicate with Stan or even Toby. But you did not make midnight phone calls in those days and, while sneaking out was something Toby might have done, it was not something I'd ever tried.

I'd never had a class with Senorita Gloria, because she taught Spanish and my father had prodded me into Latin—the language of the classics, which was taught by crabby old Mrs. Krech, who'd probably been a witness to Caesar's assassination. Originally, she'd taught Spanish, too, but a couple of years before the school had hired Senorita Gloria. I'd heard Mrs. Krech was unhappy with the arrangement, but if she communicated her displeasure to Senorita Gloria, the new Spanish teacher never showed it. Always smiling, she seemed full of energy and love of life. I'd only spoken to her once and that was when I'd collided with her rounding a hallway corner between classes, making me drop my books, but the image has stayed with me through the years—the laughing dark eyes, onyx hair, amused smile, and, most of all, the scent. It bespoke that mysterious world of jungles and hidden cities and cloud fortresses I'd seen in National

Geographic. Even at fifteen, as I watched her melt into the surge of bodies in the hall, my blood had quickened and I'd felt the stirrings of an erection.

She hadn't looked at all like the pale, pleading figure that had staggered toward me last night.

She'd wanted my help and I'd run away.

But had I really recognized her, or was it just my mind putting a face to the image now that I knew she was dead?

· · ·

The school held a special assembly that morning at nine. Dr. Cornwall, the principal, flanked by all the teachers and a thin, young priest from the campus chapel, stood in the middle of the gym at a microphone, looking grave while we sat on the benches and listened to him describe "this terrible thing" in his mellifluous voice. Students shot one another looks and whispered while he talked, and I was aware of eyes on me, as I had been aware of them throughout my first hour's math class. I looked over to find Stan, but his mother had kept him home, which left only Toby, who seemed to be enjoying a new popularity, nodding to whispered questions, and grinning behind his hand. Inexplicably, my eyes sought out Blaize, a thin, pale boy at the edge of the row just below me. He'd been kept in Saturday because he was asthmatic and now I resented the fate that had plucked him out of harm's way, when it could as easily have been he who had seen the apparition and not me.

It would only have been fair: he was taking Spanish, I wasn't.

"Incomprehensible . . ." I heard Dr. Cornwall say. ". . . dangerous place . . . irreparable loss . . . vibrant personality . . . great contribution to the school . . ."

I tried to focus on Mrs. Krech, to see if she agreed, but her face was impassive. After a final warning to report anything suspicious to him, personally, Dr. Cornwall asked the priest to come forward and say a prayer for Senorita Gloria.

When we were dismissed I started away, but Cornwall's honey-rich voice caught me.

"Colin, I need to see you for a moment."

I followed him mutely down the wax-smelling hallway like a fish being towed on a line, eyes on the ground to avoid the stares of my classmates. When we reached the office, even Mrs. O'Neil, the horse-faced secretary, looked away quickly when she saw me, as if it were not polite to make eye contact with a prisoner on his way to the chair.

Cornwall breezed into his private office, hung his gray coat on the hook, and told me to close the door and sit down.

I sank into a chair on the far side of the big, polished desk, and wondered why I was here. For a long time he stared at me through his rimless glasses, his face giving nothing away.

"Colin," he said finally, "I understand you were on the levee with some other boys Saturday night."

He said it conversationally, as you might ask someone what they thought of a movie, but something told me to be careful. He had a reputation for appearing when you least expected: in the boy's restroom when you were puffing a cigarette, behind the gym at the bike rack when two football players were squaring off, in study hall when the monitor had left for a bathroom break. Sometimes it seemed those passionless gray eyes were everywhere, and though it was unclear what the consequences of being spied out in some forbidden act were, no one wanted to make the dreaded walk to this office to find out.

"Yes, sir," I said.

"What were you doing?" he asked.

It occurred to me that it was not a school matter, and the levee was not school property, but I decided not to test him.

"Camping."

"You and who else?"

"Stan and Toby."

He considered for a moment.

"Your parents knew you were there?"

"Yes, sir." My indignation emerged more like a squeak.

"Camping." He repeated, as if rolling the word around on his tongue to savor the taste.

He picked up a silver pen with the name of the school on it and rolled it in his fingers.

"You were there all night?"

"Yes."

I waited for him to ask about Toby, but for some reason he didn't. Maybe Toby's desertion had been missed in the excitement.

"Did you see or hear anything while you were there?"

The lie slipped out unbidden. "No, sir."

"Nothing at all."

I shrugged.

"We are all shocked by what happened to Gloria—Miss Santana. I cannot tell you the depth of my own personal shock and outrage."

It came out like an accusation and I shrank in the chair.

"And I cannot tell you how much worse it is when students from my school are involved, even peripherally, in such a horrible crime."

My God, did he think we..? But he had used the word peripherally ...

"Colin, you know that if you or Stanley heard or saw anything, it is your moral duty to come forward."

"Yes, sir."

He nodded, as if it were settled. "So if you remember anything you'll come to this office."

"Yes, sir."

"And in the meantime, I'd avoid the levee and the River Road. It isn't a good place. I'm sure your father agrees. I know that if I had a son I wouldn't want him down there, and I intend to call your father."

"My father . . . ?"

"Just to pass along my thoughts." He summoned up a rare smile and unlimbered from behind the desk, a muscular man who seemed deep into middle age but whom I now realize could hardly have been more than forty. He drifted over and draped an arm over my shoulder as I moved toward the door, but somehow it felt like a shroud.

If I had a son, he'd said, as if I'd committed a crime, or, worse, as if my father had. But he didn't have a son, because he wasn't married, and somehow I couldn't envision him ever marrying a woman, with his prim, precise ways.

Toby caught me at my locker while I was getting out my books for the next class.

"What did Cornhole want?"

"None of your business. Why didn't you come back for us?"

"I did, but then I saw the cop cars."

"So you chickened out? I thought your old man could fix things."

"Fuck you, I don't have to do anything for you. For all I knew they'd caught you and Miss Stanley sucking each other off."

"Get out of here."

He leaned forward, undeterred. "Come on, what did old Cornhole say? Is he pissed because he won't be getting any more from Gloria?"

"What do you mean?"

"Shit, you know he's been punching her every time he gets a chance. You've seen her going to his office, seen him hanging around her like a damn hound dog."

"I don't know any damned thing."

"Remember? 'Down by the river where nobody goes, there stood Santana without any clothes, along came Cornwall with his walking cane, downed his pants and out it came'?"

It was a jingle that had made the rounds of the male students (although I'd never seen the principal with a cane of any kind) but I'd never given any thought to there being any truth behind it.

"That's just talk," I told him, shutting my locker.

"You're a dumbass," Toby said with a laugh.

He turned his back and lumbered off. I watched him go, riveted by a sudden doubt. He was right. There had been talk but . . .

"Somebody ought to knock him on his ass." I heard a voice and turned to see Blaize just behind me, hollows under his dark eyes. Thin as a matchstick, though a full head taller than I, he looked like a strong puff would blow him away.

"Hey, you feeling okay today?"

"Fine. I'm serious, Colin, somebody needs to deck Toby."

I shook my head. "Nah. I feel sorry for him."

"Why? He's mean. He makes fun of people and he doesn't even care what happened."

"You're new here," I told him. "But I've known Toby since the first grade."

"So?"

"In the fifth grade," I said, "we had a Christmas party at school. Everybody picked a name to give a Christmas present and you could also give presents to anybody else you felt like— you know, your special friends. Well, Toby gave a Christmas present to everybody in the class. A slingshot for the boys and a little mirror for the girls. I guess his dad paid for it. But all he got was the present from whoever drew his name. He acted like it didn't matter, but I felt bad for him."

Blaize didn't say anything.

"Look, you want to come over after school?" he said finally. "Maybe you could help me with math. I missed Friday."

"Sure." I said it without thinking, but the truth was I didn't enjoy going to Blaize's place because his mother always hovered, firing barrages of questions, as if there were an ever-present danger that something might happen to her son. My father said it was understandable, because she was a single woman, having divorced Blaize's father years before, and having had to live on her own thereafter. He told me that single parents tended to be especially watchful because their children were all they had left.

I started down the hall but Blaize stuck to my side.

"The other night, when you guys were out there . . ."

"Yeah?"

"People are saying you saw something."

A shiver went through me and I hoped he hadn't noticed.

"People are full of shit."

"Yeah."

• • •

That afternoon, for the first time I could remember, my father picked Blaize and me up after school, so that we didn't have to hitch-hike the mile or so to the Garden District where we lived. He told me he just happened to have some time off and thought he'd drop by, but I knew it wasn't true. And when he asked me how the day had been, I told him fine, not mentioning my sudden popularity at lunch and recess, when people I'd barely nodded to in the junior and senior classes had crowded out my own classmates to ask me what had really happened that night, and what we had seen, and who we thought had committed the crime. I didn't say anything about the apparition, of course, or even about how we went up on the levee looking for Toby.

Nor did I say how many times I saw Toby in the center of little crowds, as he explained to his listeners how he'd been up there with us and thought he'd heard a scream, but how sometimes you couldn't tell a human yell from that of a screech owl, which was true enough. I'd even heard him regaling them with details, supposedly gleaned from his father, of how Gloria Santana had been stabbed numerous times and how the police had already picked up a black man for questioning.

After my father let us off at our house I called Stan, but there was no answer.

I turned to Blaize.

"Look, maybe we could study over here."

He nodded at once, and I sensed that he was as eager as I was to avoid his mother's suffocating influence.

"Let me call," he said, and I listened while he explained on the phone and promised that everything would be fine.

But nobody had counted on Toby.

CHAPTER SEVEN

The next morning, after breakfast, I drive to the part of town where Gloria Santana lived. It was just north of campus, a shady middle-class neighborhood of frame houses between Nicholson Drive and Highland Road, and the picture of a green ranch-style house sticks in my mind. But as I cruise the streets I realize that I may never find it: the neighborhood has changed. The older white residents have died or moved out and the neighborhood is now primarily black. The colors of houses are different, others have been leveled, and in the place where I thought her house stood is a two-story brick apartment complex, abandoned and falling to ruin.

Or was her place a block over, on Aster?

I slow before a row of one-story frame structures, drawing curious stares, and nudge the curb in the middle of the block.

The house across the street, with weeds in the yard. It is pink now, but colors change. Still, it seems to face the wrong way, with the carport on the left.

Or can I trust my memory? Isn't that, after all, why I am here?

• • •

We didn't have any problem with memory that afternoon.

Toby said he just wanted to cruise the block, see where she lived. Nobody had invited him to my house but here he was, in my driveway, motor running, cigarette dangling from his mouth, tapping the horn until I came out to tell him to stop the noise.

"I promised to help Blaize with his math," I told him.

"This won't take a half hour," Toby said, flipping ash into the driveway. "I found out from my old man where she lived."

"It was in the newspaper," I said.

"Screw you then. Come on, Blaize, he doesn't have to go. Just you and me. I won't tell your mama."

Blaize colored. "Leave my mother out of it."

"Then stay."

Blaize looked at me. "Colin . . ."

"Fifteen fucking minutes," Toby said. "Or do the two of you want to be alone together?"

"Shut the fuck up," I said.

"Okay. I was gonna tell you about the man they arrested, but if you two fairies would rather jerk each other off . . ."

"Who?" I asked. "What's his name?"

"Get in," Toby said.

I hesitated, then gave a little shrug. "Come on, Blaize, we can go over the math when we get back."

I got into the front seat, but Blaize huddled in the back as if he was afraid someone would see him. Toby laughed to himself and shot backward down the driveway, almost hitting the median. He peeled out down the quiet street.

"So who was it?" I asked him.

"Who what?"

"The man they arrested."

"A nigger lives on the River Road. I don't know his name."

"I heard that much already. You said you knew more about him."

"He's a nigger, shithead. What's there to know? He raped her ass and then he killed her, and he's gonna fry."

I heard Blaize give a little gasp in the back seat.

"He raped her?" I asked.

"Shit, yes. What did you think this was all about?"

"How do you know?" Blaize asked then, his voice trembling.

"I know because my old man said so. He talked to the chief deputy."

"But what would she have been doing down on the River Road at night?" I asked.

"Maybe he took her there. Or maybe she was parked there, waiting for somebody, like Cornhole. Shit, she was probably screwing half the town."

"Is that something else your father told you?" I asked.

"He didn't have to. Are you so queer you didn't notice the way she used to shake it when she walked?"

"Let's go back," Blaize said.

"Fuck you," Toby said, annoyed. "We're almost there."

As soon as we turned into the street we could see the police cars, a white marked unit at the curb, manned by a single uniformed officer, and a black unmarked car in the drive. It was the first time I'd seen where she lived and now, with the yellow crime scene tape and a couple of sweating men in neckties tramping around her yard I had the sense that I was looking at a Hollywood set, where actors were going through the motions.

"What are they looking for?" Blaize asked. "I thought you said they caught the killer."

"It's what cops do," Toby said. "Like maybe he broke in and left something when he raped her."

"You mean they'll search the whole house and all her things?" Blaize asked.

"Of course."

"But what if she has private things? I mean, it doesn't seem right."

"It's a fucking murder, dumbass. Everything's fair. Besides, what if they come up with some letters from old Cornhole, say? That'd be great."

"I still don't think it's right," Blaize said, hunching deeper down in the seat.

"And you still don't have one damn reason to suspect Cornwall," I told him, though, after my visit with the principal that morning, I was starting to think the prospect might be satisfying.

"We'll see," Toby said, tossing his butt out the window.

"Where are you going?" Blaize asked, as Toby jerked the wheel into a second right turn.

"I'm making the block again. Maybe we'll see 'em bring something out."

But all we saw was the uniformed cop at the curb, who squinted up at us as we cruised slowly past.

"He's gonna come after us," I said.

"Screw him," Toby said. "It's a free country."

But the cop didn't follow, probably because the curious had been driving past all day, and a few seconds later we reached Nicholson Drive, the boulevard that connected the campus with downtown. But instead of turning right, toward the downtown area, Toby went left, toward the university.

"This isn't the way home," Blaize said.

"I'll take you home," Toby promised. "But there's one more place I want to go."

"What are you talking about?" I asked.

"I want to drive out to where it happened," he said. "It won't take long."

"Hey," I protested, "you told us . . ."

Toby glowered. "Shit on you. I just want to drive past the god-damned place."

"I want to get out," Blaize said.

"Then get the fuck out but I'm not stopping."

"You asshole," Blaize swore.

"Just for that I may make you walk back from the cemetery. How'd you like that, mama's boy? What would your old lady say then?"

Blaize lunged from the back seat and Toby ducked. The car swerved into the next lane and Toby cursed.

"You skinny little bastard, if you make me wreck, I'll beat the piss out of you."

"Go back now," I said. "I'll beat the piss out of you if you don't."

But he only accelerated.

"You won't do shit unless you want to get us all killed."

"You mother fucker," I said.

"Yeah, sure." We came to the River Road and Toby whipped through the stop sign onto the gravel. We skidded and then he straightened out, leaving a spray of rocks and dust behind us. Now the levee was on our right, and there were open pastures on the left. My heart started to beat faster. I didn't want to go back to the place and yet, at the same time, there was a thrill I couldn't deny.

We rounded a curve and on the right I saw Bergeron's store, a ramshackle wooden structure with a tin roof, a couple of propane tanks on the side, and two gas pumps in front. Toby eased off the accelerator.

"Come on, ladies, I'll buy us Cokes."

We eased to a stop at the side of the building and Toby opened his door.

"You people coming?"

I opened my door and, grudgingly, Blaize opened his. At least we were on safe ground. Alcide Bergeron was a friend, someone we'd bought soft drinks and foodstuffs from on our camping trips, and who'd let us use his phone when we needed to call our parents to be picked up. He lived behind the store, in a couple of added-on rooms, with his wife and four kids, all girls. There was a fifth daughter, grown up now and married, and sometimes we saw her at the store, visiting, with a baby in her arms. But it was the second-to-oldest daughter, Michelle, that we all noticed.

She was a senior in high school, dark and lush, and mysterious. We'd speculated endlessly during our nights in camp as to whether her fruit had been plucked. Stan doubted it, I didn't know, and Toby said it was a foregone conclusion, though, for once, he made no claims of firsthand knowledge. Now, as we drifted into the store, we saw her at the far end of the counter, breasts thrusting against her white parochial school blouse. She glanced casually up from a schoolbook and then dismissed us as if we were of no consequence.

"Boys," Alcide Bergeron said, getting up from behind the counter where he was watching a tiny black-and-white television.

We mumbled greetings and went past the dusty shelves of mostly stale bread and outdated canned goods to the cooler, where we delved for our drinks. From the living quarters in back came the smell of grease frying and I thought I heard the clink of a skillet.

Toby leaned toward me as he extracted a Coca Cola and whispered: "Did you see the way she looked at us when we came in? Hot . . ."

I moved away with my Dr. Pepper.

"You boys down here the other night?" Bergeron asked genially. He was somewhere in his forties, with wrinkled skin and receding hair, stocky and on the verge of running to fat.

"Yeah, but we didn't see anything," I said quickly.

"No." He seemed amused. "Well, that was a hell of a thing." He leaned forward over the counter. "You boys know this woman?"

I nodded. Toby said: "Blaize here had a class with her."

"Damn." Bergeron shook his head. "I hear she was a nice-looking woman."

There was a rustle of curtains at the far end of the store and Mrs. Bergeron, a fat woman with an enormous bosom, emerged into the store area and I figured she'd been listening all along.

"It's not safe any more," she said. "I worry about all of us."

"They caught the man did it," Toby said. "A nigger."

Alcide Bergeron snorted. "Amos Poole didn't kill nobody. He barely has enough sense to come in out the rain. Fact is, they let him loose this morning, 'cause I saw him just an hour ago. He come in here for his pork and beans."

Toby blinked, caught up short.

"Must of been another nigger," he said finally.

"Hell," Bergeron said, "wasn't no nigger."

Mrs. Bergeron interrupted then, shooing her daughter into the back room.

"Michelle, you got no need to hear this. You got studying anyway."

But before Michelle vanished she cast a sultry glance in our direction and I was certain she was looking directly at me.

"I know who done it," the storekeeper said.

For a few seconds the only sound came from the television. Then Toby spoke.

"You saw?"

"Didn't need to see," Bergeron pronounced. "I know. Who else could've done it but Rufus Sikes, the no-count bastard."

"Sikes," I said.

"Hell, yes. I wouldn't put nothing past that man. I won't have him in my store and I've told him to keep away from my family.

I see him around here . . ." Bergeron reached down and brought up a rifle. "I'll do what the law should of done a long time ago."

"But you didn't actually see him," Toby said.

"Son, you some kind of lawyer or something? I told you, now don't be smart."

I broke in before Toby got us all thrown out.

"We saw a car," I said.

Bergeron blinked. "You mean the other night?"

"We were up on the levee," I said. "We saw a car heading down the River Road. Of course, it may not've had anything to do with it."

The storekeeper shrugged. "Cars always going up and down the River Road at night. College students, mostly. Yeah, I heard a car about midnight. I'd just had it out with that girl of mine for dragging in late again. I thought it was that boy coming back to sneak her out and I was gonna tell him a thing or two." He shook his head. "Young people these days: my old man would've whipped my ass if I come in at that hour. You kids don't know what you do to your parents, you."

But I wasn't thinking about the worried storekeeper, I was thinking about Michelle and wondering if she'd really been home all night. Maybe she had snuck out again. Maybe Toby had been right about her. Maybe she'd ended up with her boy-friend, in the backseat of his car, or at some motel, or at his parents' house while they were away. What would she look like with her clothes off? I tried to envision her but failed.

"Let's go," Toby said, setting his empty bottle on the counter.

Bergeron nodded. "You boys take it easy. Stay away from Sikes, you hear?"

We nodded and went back out to Toby's car.

"Let's get back to town," Blaize said.

"We will," Toby said. "I just want to drive past the graveyard, since we're already out here."

It didn't do any good to argue, because he was already turning left, away from town. I sat back, gritting my teeth. I didn't really want to go there, I told myself, and yet in a sense I did. I wanted to see it in daylight, convince myself that I'd only imagined the specter of the other night. And maybe when we got there the place would be deserted and it would be like nothing had happened at all.

We came to Windsong, a brooding hulk half-hidden by an alley of live oaks and pecan trees. The iron gate was locked, as it always was, and the grass on the lawn was ankle high. Behind it were the outlines of outbuildings, and behind them, a half-mile from the River Road, the massive brick finger of the smokestack that was all that remained of the sugarhouse. It was hard to imagine bygone revels or women in *Gone With the Wind* attire gracing the porch and lawn, especially when we passed the shack that served as the home for the overseer, Rufus Sikes.

A 1950 Belair on blocks decorated the grassless front yard and chickens pecked futilely at the dirt. A barefoot boy of five with corn-colored hair stared at us as we passed and then spat in our direction, but the master of the manor was nowhere in evidence.

I thought about what Alcide Bergeron had said about Sikes being the killer. I didn't know if it was true, but I wanted it to be.

"Shit," Toby said, and I turned to the road in front of us. Ahead, at the place where the dirt track led back to the cemetery, a white sheriff's unit blocked the entrance. "The bastards have it blocked off."

"Why don't you stop and tell 'em who your father is?" Blaize said.

Toby's knuckles turned white on the steering wheel. "You skinny little mother, I oughta put your ass out right now."

"He's right," I said. "You brought us all the way here."

"Fuck you both," Toby growled. "You want to see the place? Okay. I'll take you where you can see it."

"What are you talking about?" I asked, but I knew. Toby gunned forward to an open gate on the side of the levee and wheeled off the gravel and up the grassy slope.

"Oh, Jesus," I said. "You're gonna get us stuck up here." I had visions of explaining to my father and of the hysterics Blaize's mother would surely throw.

"Nobody's getting stuck," Toby said, bumping onto the top of the dike. He jerked the wheel right and we were on the little track that led along the top of the levee all the way back to the city. "We can see from right up here."

We bounced over a rut and a clot of cattle moved slowly out of the way. Just ahead a fence led up one side of the levee and then down the other, but there was no gate to bar the road, just a wooden sign: NO TRESPASSING. PROPERTY OF WINDSONG PLANTATION.

"You aren't going through there?" Blaize asked.

"Watch me. Nobody owns the levee. My old man told me. Only people that can kick us off here are the levee police."

Blaize said something under his breath and I knew what he was thinking. You hardly ever saw the levee police and somebody like Rufus Sikes didn't give a damn about them anyway.

Still, it wasn't but half a mile and we were already well into it. There was no place to turn around so we might as well just keep going. A few minutes more and we'd be out of the forbidden zone and it wouldn't matter.

I allowed myself to glance out over the fields, in the direction of the cemetery, but all I could see was a second white car parked at the grove of trees that marked the gravestones.

Then another thought came to me and my stomach did a little flip. What if I'd left footmarks in the dry dirt of the cemetery road? What if I'd dropped something when I tripped? How could I explain myself if somehow they found out I'd been there?

Then I remembered what Toby had said once: The cops around here are bozos. My old man said they couldn't find their dicks with both hands. The only way they solve crimes is somebody confesses or squeals on somebody.

I didn't know if it was true, but I could hope.

But why should I be worried? I hadn't done anything and there were plenty of better suspects. Rufus Sikes, for example. Surely they'd be talking to him.

I saw Windsong below. From the levee top I could see the distant fields better, make out the tumbled pile of brick that was the old sugar refinery.

I was shaken out of my thoughts by Toby leaning on the horn. In front of us a herd of cattle blocked the road, milling about with no apparent concern for the automobile. Toby hit the horn again and a couple of the cows raised their heads.

"Get the hell out the way!" Toby cursed but the animals seemed not to hear. He jerked open his door and got out, waving his hands at them. "Get on, damn you."

He started forward, shooing the cattle, and maybe that was why he didn't hear, but we did, through the open door: it was the rumble and clank of another vehicle, coming up from behind us, and when I turned my head to look through the rearview window my blood went cold.

It was a battered red Ford pickup, with a shattered right headlight and the front bumper hanging at an angle, like it had hit one pedestrian too many. I'd seen that truck before, in the front yard of the Sikes shack.

"Jesus, Toby . . ." I yelled, but it was too late. Like the mummy in the old movies, the truck inched toward us, its progress infinitely slow but inevitable. Then it was stopping and the driver's door was opening and when Toby turned around I saw all the color drain out of his face.

The man who limped toward us wore faded overalls and his face was the color of raw hamburger. A felt hat shaded bead-like eyes and he carried a tire tool in his left hand.

"Christ," Blaize breathed. Toby took two quick steps forward, then ducked into the car, slammed the door and reached for the shift lever, but by then it was too late.

Sikes was already leaning over the open car window, his foul breath filling the inside of the car like a pestilential fog.

"What're you boys doing up here?" he demanded in a raspy voice.

Toby cleared his throat. "Just taking a shortcut."

"Shortcut to where? Can't you read signs? You're trespassing. You're on Windsong. I can have you locked up."

"We just want to leave," Toby said, his voice unaccustomedly meek. "But the cattle . . ."

"I seen what you was doing with the cattle. Scaring 'em. Trying to run 'em away. Cattle get spooked, they take off, run into fences, trip down and break their legs. Drown in the borrow pit."

Toby's mouth opened but no words came out.

"I found a cow last month with a broke leg. Somebody run into her. Had to shoot her. Three hundred dollars. You got three hundred dollars?"

"Mister, it wasn't us," Toby swore.

"That's what you say," Sikes said, leering through rotten teeth. "How do I know? People would hit one of my cows would lie."

"I'm not lying, I swear."

"Who's your daddy, boy?"

"He works downtown," Toby squeaked.

"One of them state workers, huh?"

"Yes, sir, I guess."

"You guess. You know about that woman they found down there the other night?"

Behind me I heard Blaize's breath leak out.

"She was where she didn't have no business being," the overseer said before Toby could answer. "You boys got no business being here, neither. You want to end up the same way?"

Toby swallowed. "We didn't do anything . . ."

"Don't tell me what you didn't do. I know all about you city kids from rich families, coming down here with girls, drinking, raising hell . . ."

Toby started to say something but I nudged him with my knee.

"I ought to teach you all a lesson," Sikes said. "But I'll let you go this time. You're lucky it was me, though: If it was Mr. Drood caught you, you'd wish you'd never come."

The evil visage vanished from the window and I heard him calling to the cows, shooing them out of the way. As he stumped toward them, the herd parted and Toby popped the clutch. The car shot forward, skidding and then straightening as we reached the open gate that marked the end of Windsong property.

Behind us the herd had reformed in the center of the levee and Toby slowed, leaning his head out of the window.

"You red-necked mother fucker!" he yelled back in Sikes' direction. "Fuck you and your fucking cows!"

"You stupid bastard," I cried. "What the hell are you trying to do?"

"He can't catch us now," Toby said, wiping what looked suspiciously like sweat off his forehead. "I'm damned if some white trash piece of shit's gonna run me off public property."

"Let's just go home," Blaize said quietly.

Toby found the road that led down the levee toward Bergeron's store and a few seconds later we were back on the gravel and headed for town.

He didn't say another word until we reached my house.

CHAPTER EIGHT

I sit in front of the house where I grew up, on Cherokee Street, in the shade of the water oaks, and try to remember how it was. My parents bought the house when I was five and I lived there until I went away to college. It is a bungalow with brick pillars and a screened-in front porch with a swing, but the swing is gone and I have the urge to get out, knock on the door, and demand where it is. There is a light in the front bedroom window but since it is mid-morning, I think it unlikely anyone is at home. Maybe if I went up the walk, knocked on the door, it would magically open, and when I looked inside everything would be the same as it was then, but, of course, I know better,

I close my eyes and try to see myself as a six-year-old, running across the lawn to get the afternoon paper for my father, so it will be on the coffee table when he comes in from the university. I smell cookies baking and hear my mother humming in the kitchen. It is an idyllic scene, something I have fixed on over and over throughout the years but now, for the first time, I begin to wonder if it ever really happened, or whether it is just the way I wanted things to be.

Then I think about when I was seven and playing in the shed behind the house and my mother called me to come in, and how I listened to the sound of her voice, the change in tone from merely questioning, then the rising note of aggravation and finally the high pitch of fear, and I recall the pleasure at know-ing that I could stay here as long as I wanted, and that when I came out, it would be a relief to her and she would love me all the more, because she would see I was all right. And so I stayed in the cobwebs, surrounded by the dank smell of earth, huddling among the garden tools, and saw the door open, a brief square of light, and heard her call my name, and still I said nothing. By that time I realized it was too late, that soon my father would be home and if I came out now he would be called on to discipline me, though the fear was worse than anything he had ever actu-ally done.

So I stayed, by now thoroughly frightened, until I decided that if I ran away, maybe I could escape, but I'd only gotten half-way down the alley behind the house, that served as a route for the garbage trucks, when a neighbor saw me, and seconds later, as I reached the cross street, my father's blue car was stopping, blocking the alley and the door was opening, and he was jerking me inside.

But I needn't have worried, because they were so glad to see me that all was forgiven, and afterwards I felt guilty. Later my mother explained that before I was born I'd almost had a brother or sister, but she'd miscarried, and she and my father had grieved over the miscarriage, and that they couldn't stand the thought of losing a child again, and though I was not sure until much later what a miscarriage was, I knew that they loved me very much.

Maybe that was why I decided I could get away with things.

Her name was Leslie, and she was a year younger than I was and lived next door, and one day I invited her into the shed while we were playing in the backyard and I convinced her to undress and she let me look between her legs and then I showed her my own organ and we did that several more times until one day I called for her to come play and found out that she couldn't come any more. That day my mother told me about how boys and girls were different, which was something I'd realized long before Leslie, though I hadn't been entirely certain just how, and she explained how there were some things people didn't do, and she told me that Leslie wouldn't be coming again, but that she knew I hadn't realized I was doing anything wrong, but not to do it again.

I wondered where Leslie was now, the little straw-haired girl whose face I barely remembered, who so unselfconsciously spread herself for me and let me look into the folds of her six-year-old flesh. Did she even remember? Did she laugh about it with her husband? Her own daughters? Was she even still alive? How many lovers had she had, and would she even still remember my name?

When I was eight my parents planned a vacation. Now, we'd had vacations before. In 1950 we went to Florida, where we took a glass-bottomed boat and saw nature gardens and swam in the Gulf. But this was to be a super vacation, all the way to Michigan, which was where my father's family lived. There'd been much discussion over whether he could afford to not teach summer school and finally he'd convinced my mother that it was something he had to do, because though they'd married during the war, many of his family had never met her and none of them had seen me, and when would they ever get another chance?

I think she, as a girl from Louisiana, was afraid of what they would think of her, because ours was a backward state, which, until Huey Long, had barely had any paved roads or bridges, and people in the north thought of it as almost another country. I remember that they argued bitterly because he said that it was a long way to drive and went out and bought a new car.

It was the only time I could remember their arguing, but the ferocity of it stayed in my mind forever afterwards.

It started when he brought it home, a new blue Pontiac. I remember staring at it, excited. As long as I'd been alive the family had limped along in a '39 Ford, and Mr. Ruggles, the mechanic at the Esso Station, on Dufroq Street, had almost been a member of the family. My father even kept a bicycle for those days when the car was out of commission and he had no other means to get to work. Dad said Mr. Ruggles had a drinking problem, and sometimes he didn't show up for a couple of days, but when he did, he could fix anything with wheels. But now, he proudly explained, as I stood wonderingly on the lawn, Mr. Ruggles and the bike could be consigned to the past. The new car was dark blue, sleek, with an Indian head ornament on the hood, and my father said proudly that it would go a hundred miles an hour.

Then Mother came out.

"Look!" I told her, sharing my father's happiness, but as soon as I saw her face I knew things were about to crash.

I'll never forget the stricken look.

"Charles, you didn't . . ." The words choked in her throat and my father's sudden ebullience seemed to fragment.

"We're going to spend every cent we ever saved to go on this jaunt this summer and you turn around and buy a new car?"

"We've never had one," he said, his voice weak in a way I'd never heard it before. "I didn't have to put much money down and the payments . . ."

"We can barely afford the payments on the house now," Mother said. "My God, Charles . . ."

"Evelyn, we were spending more on the old car than we'll pay in notes on this one. It was in the garage every week."

"But a Pontiac? You couldn't even get a Chevrolet. You had to get the most expensive car they make."

"The most expensive is a Cadillac," he said quietly.

She didn't answer, just ran into the house. For a tortured second his eyes met mine and I saw the disappointment. Then he rushed after her.

I stood on the lawn, paralyzed. I'd never known them to argue before. Sure, sometimes she'd complained about one thing or another and he'd get a pained tone in his voice, but it always seemed to die away. But now I heard their raised voices, from inside.

She was yelling at him, and I heard words like "bills" and "poor house," and "expensive toy." I put my hands against my ears, but then I felt foolish and I thought the neighbors might see and wonder what I was doing, so I crept around the side of the house, out of sight of the street. I was just outside their bedroom and I heard the door slam and the springs of the bed squeak, as if someone had landed on it, and then I heard his voice, muffled, as if coming from the hallway outside:

". . . just wanted us to be safe . . . don't want to break down on some road in Mississippi . . ."

His words were blotted out by her crying and I realized she was lying on the bed.

Maybe, I thought, if I hadn't been standing there when he'd driven up, hadn't shown delight at the new vehicle, maybe then he'd have had a chance to explain to her and this wouldn't have happened. For a long time I waited, trying to make up my mind whether to go inside, try to explain, tell them it was my fault. Or whether I should just leave, for good this time, go somewhere they'd never find me again, where I wouldn't make any more trouble. Maybe, I thought, if I ran into the street and let a car run over me, or went to the river and jumped off the ferry. But after what seemed forever her sobbing grew more muffled, so that I could barely hear it, and I wondered if she was all right, and I guess my father wondered, too, because after a while I heard the door open and footsteps and then I heard his voice, low and soothing, and she gave out a few more sobs, and the only words I could make out were his saying something about taking the car back, but she said she didn't want that, and after a time I heard the bed squeak again, and then they were talking in low voices and she said something about locking the door, and I heard his footsteps, padding this time, as if he'd taken off his shoes, and a while later I heard the bed start to squeak rhythmically and heard her gasping and I thought he must be doing something to her but I wasn't sure what.

That night, at dinner, they were quieter than usual but there was no mention of the car or of vacation and I didn't know what had been decided because two days later she was dead.

Years later, when I thought about it, I realized I'd never really known what had happened, only what I'd been told by people who'd wanted to shield me. What they said was that she'd been downtown shopping, had stepped off a curb, and been hit by a car. A freak thing, something that happened every day, and because I was young, people wanted to protect me from the hurt. But because they said as little as possible, in later years it came to be imbued with a mysterious quality. Why had she been downtown that Tuesday morning? Her usual shopping day was Saturday. She'd had to take a bus downtown because Father had the car. Of course, she might have been shopping for our trip. But I never heard what she'd had with her when she'd been found. All I remembered was my father's ashen face and the way he'd sleepwalked through the next few weeks and months. We didn't take the vacation, of course, and six months after it happened he sold the Pontiac and got a second-hand Dodge. For a long time her clothes stayed in their bedroom, and nothing was changed. It was as if she were still living there and one day would walk in the door. Five years after she died, when I was in junior high, he dated a couple of times, women whom he'd met at the university, but nothing ever came of it. Years later, when I'd finished college and was on my own, he remarried, but I'd long since made my own life. Maybe it was the memory of that fight they'd had so soon before she'd died, and the thought that my father must have carried that with him for the rest of his life, like a millstone.

But then, I tell myself, seated in front of the old house, my parents weren't the only ones who had disagreements. Stan's parents had had a hell of a fight the afternoon Toby and Blaize and I came back from the confrontation with Sikes on the levee.

Toby dropped us at my house and I helped Blaize for a while with his homework, though neither of us had our minds on it after what had happened with Sikes.

"Do you think he really did it?" Blaize asked.

"I dunno. But he sure had Toby shitting in his drawers."

I walked Blaize home and his mother jerked open the apartment door before he was halfway up the steps.

"Are you all right?" She reminded me of the Wicked Witch of the West, tall, angular and dark, but, unlike the witch, she was always festooned with jewelry and exuded a perfume that made me want to sneeze. My father said she came from old family and had married a man who hadn't acted responsibly—those were his words. Toby said Blaize's father had been a drunk and wrote bad checks, and that they divorced because he'd spent all her money. The only product of the marriage was Blaize, sickly and diffident. Two years ago, Blaize had come to our school, and the rumor was that Blanche St. Martin had badgered politicians and university administrators until they'd made room for her son at the laboratory school, which was a protected environment catering to the affluent, well-connected, and the children of university faculty.

"Colin, would you come in for a moment?" she asked, and hustled me inside, as if she didn't want anyone to see us together.

I followed slowly, eyes peeled for flying monkeys.

She shut the door behind us. It was stuffy in the room, but I don't know whether it was the lack of air conditioning or just the fact that the room smelled like mothballs and Lysol.

"Sit down," she said. She pointed to a straight-backed chair to insure that I wouldn't choose one of the antique, stuffed monstrosities that, so far as I could tell, nobody was allowed to sit in.

I took my seat and caught a look of sympathy from Blaize.

"Blaize, darling, go into the kitchen and get the cookies off the stove, will you?" she asked.

A few seconds later Blaize shuffled back in with a plate of blackened objects.

"They got a little overdone," Blanche said. "But it doesn't hurt to be too careful." She nodded at Blaize. "Pass some to Colin, dear."

I took one. It felt like a rock and I held it, unsure what to do.

"You know, I called your father's home," Blanche said, her voice kindly but accusing. "There was no answer."

"We must have been outside," I said quickly.

"Studying outside?" she asked, penciled brows arching.

"We went down to the drugstore, too," I lied.

"I see."

I raised the stone-like cookie to my mouth, pretended to eat some, but it tasted like charcoal.

"It's good," I mumbled.

"You know, Colin, this is not a very nice world that we live in." She sighed and touched her hair bun. "It's not the world I remember when I was growing up. In those days, you could hitch hike a ride and never have to worry. Tramps came to the door and you always fed them. Things just didn't *happen*."

"No, ma'am."

"But these days . . ." Another sigh. "You understand why I don't encourage Blaize going down to the levee."

"Yes, ma'am."

"It's not you boys. You're good boys. I know you come from good stock. But you're so young. None of you really understand what it's like in this world today."

There isn't anything much you can say to something like that. She took the plate from the coffee table and thrust it at me.

"Aren't you going to eat another one? Oh, well, I guess it *is* close to supper. I wouldn't want your father to be upset with me. Such a sweet man. I hope you appreciate what a wonderful father you have, Colin. To do such a splendid job rearing a boy like you, all by himself. A Negro maid is no substitute for a mother. I know he misses her. I'm sure you do, too."

I wasn't sure what to say. I suppose I missed her, but in kids' years it had been a long time and all I had were the jumbled images.

"You've been so kind to Blaize. I know that's your rearing showing, it always does, you know. Blaize was so mistreated at the public school. Children can be so cruel."

Blaize looked down at the rug and I knew he wished he could blend into it.

"Some of those boys were just toughs. Common. And some of the girls, well . . ." She shook her head: "I thought it would be better at the Catholic school, but the nuns just give no individual attention at all. I told them, 'You can't use religion as an excuse. I expect something for my money.'"

"Yes, ma'am."

"Still, I know it's been hard for Blaize at the Lab School. He didn't start out there, and I know that means a lot. That's why I'm so grateful for the way you've befriended him."

"Mom . . ." Blaize said, like he was choking on a hot poker.

"He's really a musical prodigy, you know," she went on, oblivious to her son's discomfort. "He belongs with a group that can appreciate that, not with a bunch of football players."

I tried to conceal the stone-like cookie in my fist. "I really have to go now, Mrs. St. Martin."

"Of course. I'll take you home. I wouldn't want your father to think I'd just let you walk the streets."

"Really . . ." I tried to protest but Blaize rolled his eyes and I knew I didn't have a chance. She ushered us out to the old yellow Chrysler and managed to back up onto the curb before she got it straightened out and into the street. Inside the closed car, the smell was overpowering and I realized it was the odor of lilies, as if we were part of a funeral cortege.

"You know, you're very lucky," she said, jamming the brakes suddenly as we reached the middle of the intersection with Park Boulevard, as if she'd only now noticed the stop sign. "There's no telling what could have happened to you boys on the levee that night. Not that I worry very much about that Toby. He is not the kind I like to see Blaize associate with, and I frankly am a little surprised you would go with him, Colin, but Stanley is a nice boy, from good parents, well-bred. You can always tell quality."

A car was entering the boulevard from a side street and she lurched toward the neutral ground.

"He paid no more attention to that stop sign . . . Well, no matter."

"I could walk the rest of the way," I said but she ignored me.

"The way people drive in this city, there ought to be a law." Her head swung in my direction: "How *is* Stanley? What did his mother say about what happened the other night?"

"I don't know."

"Surely you talked to him."

"He didn't come to school today."

"Oh." For a moment she seemed genuinely surprised. "Did you call?"

"Nobody answered."

"Now isn't that odd? Of course, his father's never there, that's understood. Doctors are never home, especially his kind. And maybe that's the reason . . ."

I waited, but she pursed her lips, as if determined no other word would sneak out.

We came to my house and I saw the car in the driveway, indicating my father was back from the university. A curtain moved in the front window and I knew he was watching. A few seconds later, before I could close the car door, he was striding down the sidewalk, tie flapping loose, and there was something in his face I couldn't read.

He leaned down before I could shut the door and looked in.

"How are you this evening, Blanche?"

I heard her answer, but before I could hear anything else he turned to me.

"You can go inside now, Colin. You can take out the plates and glasses for supper."

I went in, but once the front door was closed, it was my turn to peek through the front window. He was still hunched over, talking with her, and I wondered what they were saying. Nothing very secret, if Blaize was in the back seat.

Five minutes later I heard the car door shut and he came back in, his face serious. While I set the table and heated the dish that our maid, Delia, had prepared, he seemed preoccupied. Finally, after supper, he called me into the living room and packed his pipe.

"Colin, I understand that while you were camping on the levee Saturday night Toby left you and Stanley and disappeared."

I gulped. "Yes, sir."

"Is there some reason you didn't tell me this?"

I shrugged. "I guess it didn't seem important."

"No? Murders don't happen down there on the levee every day. If I'd known Toby was going to abandon you and Stanley I'd never have let you go with him."

I waited, breathing in the sweet smoke from his briar.

"So what happened, son? Did you boys have a disagreement?"

"Nothing important."

"Son, when somebody gets killed, everything's important."

"It's just Toby wanted to go into town and we wanted to stay and camp."

My father nodded, sucking on the pipe. "I should have known. What did he want to do, go get some beer? Pick up some girls?"

"Something like that," I mumbled.

He nodded. "I'm not surprised. And it's not that abnormal. There'll come a time . . ." His voice trailed off. "But not quite yet. I think it would be better if you stayed away from Toby. The boy has problems. I don't say they're of his own making. Still . . ." His head gave a little shake. "Blanche St. Martin has a way of finding out everything, and once she finds something out, everybody knows. That's why I wanted to talk to her, to head off any talk."

"Dad, she said something about Stan's dad, how he was never there, something about his kind never was, and . . ."

My father tapped his pipe on the crystal ashtray. "Well, he's in obstetrics and gynecology. Women pick the strangest times to have babies. You, for example: I took your mother to the hospital at two in the morning and you came at four."

"That was Stan's dad?"

"No, but I hear he's a fine doctor. Very popular. I'm sure it puts a strain on Stan, having his father gone so much, but that's a doctor's life. Did Blanche . . . Mrs. St. Martin . . . say anything else?"

"Like what?"

"Oh, nothing in particular. But look, son, if she does . . . Don't take it too seriously. She's had a hard time, trying to rear poor Blaize on her own, and, well, it probably gives her a certain view of the world . . ."

"You're raising me on your own. You don't have any special view."

"How do you know?" He chuckled. "Now go get on with your lessons. I have to go back out to school. We're having a special faculty meeting. I may be back late, nine or so. I want to find you ready for bed."

"Yes, sir," I said, but I knew it was a chance I couldn't let pass.

CHAPTER NINE

As soon as I heard the car leave the driveway I called Stan's number. This time his mother answered.

"Stan can't come," she snapped. "He doesn't have time to talk, goodbye." The phone went dead and I stared at it, nonplussed. I'd never heard her sound like that before. Had Stan done something that had caused him to be punished? Leaving the canoe down at the levee? Was that why he hadn't come to school today? But the deputy had said it was all right to leave the boat. What the hell was going on?

I figured there was only one way to find out.

My father had said he wouldn't be back until late, and it wasn't quite seven now, so that gave me a couple of hours. Stan's house was in College Town, three miles away on the other side of the campus. I could walk there in an hour, less if I caught a ride.

Five minutes after I stuck out my thumb I got a lift from a college boy on his way to pick up his date at Evangeline Hall. Things like that happened back then. He took me an extra couple of blocks to the South Gates and I walked the three blocks to Stan's place, the two-story Spanish home with a pool and *garconiere*, behind it, where Stan lived. He was the youngest of three brothers and when the first two had left for college, he'd moved in and now stayed there by himself, twenty yards behind the main house, a situation all of us envied.

As I walked down his drive, I saw both cars were present, and lights were on in the main house, as well as in Stan's little cabin. Something came romping out of the darkness and I steeled myself as Stan's black lab, India, jumped me, trying to wash my face with her tongue.

I pushed her away, giving her head a pat, and I continued toward the backyard. The canoe, I noticed, was in its usual place, on two sawhorses, beside the little dwelling. I walked around it to the front of the cabin. The door was closed and I heard the radio blasting "Sea of Love."

I started to knock, then changed my mind and pressed my face against the window.

Stan lay face down on the bed, not moving. I thought at first he might be sick but he was fully dressed, and his books were on the floor, as if he'd been studying. But there was something about his posture that seemed unnatural. I moved to the door and knocked.

No answer, so I knocked harder.

Seconds later I heard his muffled voice.

"Go away."

"Hey, Stan, it's me, Colin."

No answer, then there was a movement at the window. Then the door opened a crack and I started forward but he made no move to let me in.

"What do you want?"

His face was drawn, as if he were ill, and wetness streaked his cheeks.

"Hey, man, what's wrong?"

"Nothing. Just leave me alone, okay?"

"Stan . . ."

"*Please . . .*"

It was like he was begging, and it took me by surprise. I shrugged.

"Sure."

He closed the door again and I stood outside for a long time, battered by the loud music.

I'd never seen him like that and I didn't know what to do. But after I'd stood there for five minutes I knew he wasn't going to change his mind, so I turned and started back up the driveway. I'd only gotten halfway when I heard the voices.

Somebody inside, a woman, was screaming. At first I thought it was the TV and then I realized, with shock, that it was Stan's mother. I couldn't hear what she was saying but every few seconds, when she paused for breath, I heard a low mumble that I knew must be Stan's father, answering.

I stood rooted, not sure what to do. I had no idea what the argument was about and I'd never heard either of them raise their voices before, though Mrs. Chandler frequently seemed haggard, as if she hadn't gotten enough rest. As for Dr. Chandler, I hardly saw him at all.

I waited a few more minutes, wondering if I should go back to comfort Stan, but I finally decided there wasn't anything I could do, so I started forward again. When I got to the edge of the house, though, the front door flew open. Dr. Benson Chandler hurtled toward me, head down, and I flattened myself against the side of the house, feeling the bushes stick my skin.

"Go on!" his wife yelled, following him out the door. "Go to whichever one it is now, you bastard. But this time don't come slinking back."

Chandler jerked open his car door and a second later the engine roared to life. The car rocketed backward, toward the street, and I saw Helen Chandler silhouetted, her back to me as she faced the street, fist upraised. The car leapt into gear and then shot away down the street, without headlights. For another second Helen Chandler's fist remained raised and then it fell limply to her side, as if she was giving up. She turned and walked slowly back into the house.

I waited until I was sure she wasn't coming out again and then I hurried off, keeping to the shadows as I made my way up to Stanford Avenue, in case Dr. Chandler have second thoughts and come home.

That night I lay awake for hours, trying to make sense of what had happened. Married people argued, but even when my mother and father had argued on that long-ago day when he'd bought the car, there hadn't been name calling. I wondered what Stan's father had done. And I wondered if Stan would be at school tomorrow. I hoped he would, and then I hoped he wouldn't, because how could I look him in the face? Of course, he didn't know I'd heard his parents arguing, but I doubted I could keep it from him. All he'd have to do was look at my face.

When I finally drifted off to sleep I dreamed of the screaming voices, only this time when the doctor came rushing out of the house I didn't make it into the bushes quickly enough and he saw me. And as I tried to melt into the side of the house I realized the man coming toward me with upraised fist wasn't Dr. Benson Chandler at all: It was Rufus Sikes.

CHAPTER TEN

But the next day Stan was at school and when I saw him between classes he acted as if nothing had happened. He sought me out at lunch.

"You think you could come over after school?"

I shrugged. "I reckon. Is everything okay?"

"Fine. I was sick yesterday is all.'"

When school ended, Toby appeared at my locker:

"What's the story with Stanley? Was he really sick?"

"What do you mean really?"

"Come on, let's go for a ride."

"I can't."

"Why?"

"I have something to do."

"Like what? You going to fairy boy's house?"

"I told you Blaize isn't a fairy."

"Fuck you, man, I can tell one when I see one."

I left him laughing and made my way out to the parking lot, where Stan and I were supposed to meet. He'd said his mother was going to pick us up and I wanted to hurry, before Toby saw us. But I was too late, because as Stan and I got into the station wagon I saw Toby watching from the sidewalk.

"How are you today, Colin?" Stan's mother asked. She was trying to sound upbeat but I couldn't get last night's memory out of my mind.

"Fine."

"I hope you didn't think I was abrupt on the phone yesterday. Stanley wasn't feeling well and I was worried."

I nodded and Stan looked away.

"I'm fine," Stan said. "I just wanted to show you my last *Guns and Ammo*. There's a Ruger in there I'd like to get."

"Of course," his mother said.

When we got to the house we went to Stan's cabin.

"It's not true about the *Guns and Ammo*, is it?" I asked.

"No. They wouldn't let me have a pistol anyway."

"So?" I flopped in his chair and waited. He looked from the Yogi Berra poster on the wall to the LSU pennant, licking his lips.

"Nothing. I just wanted to know what went on at school yesterday."

"That's why you didn't want to talk to me last night?"

"Colin, for God's sake, please leave it alone . . ."

"Sure." I went over to the bookcase, picked up the plastic model P-51 Mustang. "Well, Cornwall called me in, and I guess he talked to Toby, too—wanted to know if we saw anything."

"Yeah, he talked to me today, too. But what were the kids saying about what happened?"

I shrugged. "Nobody knew what to say, except Toby. He said Cornwall and Senorita Gloria were screwing."

"That fat, red-headed fuck."

"Yeah. But she did have a way, you know? I mean, you got to admit, even if she was as old as she was, you wouldn't have minded getting a piece."

"You're full of shit," Stan said. "She was a teacher, damn it."

"Yeah, I know, but I mean, look, suppose she wasn't a teacher and you just met her somewhere. Are you telling me you wouldn't put it in her if she gave you the go-ahead?"

"No, goddamn it."

I could see it wouldn't do any good to argue. After all, he wasn't the one who'd run into her in the hallway that day at school, smelled her perfume, stared down her cleavage as she bent to help me pick up my books, and watched her hips sway as she walked away.

"Only other thing is we went up on the levee after school with Toby."

"What?" He straightened on the bed, frowning. "You went back there with him?"

"Me and Blaize." I told him about going by Gloria's home, and then the visit to Bergeron's store, and what Bergeron had said about Sikes most likely being the killer.

"But he didn't even know her," Stan said.

"He didn't have to. Maybe she went there to wait for somebody, Cornwall, say, and Sikes just came along. Then, when Cornwall came and found her, he took off."

"Maybe." He pursed his lips. "But I just don't think she'd do something like that."

"What do you mean?"

"They're teachers."

"And teachers don't fuck?"

"I didn't say that. I just don't think she would. I had her for homeroom last year. She just wasn't that way."

"How the hell would you know?"

"You have to believe in some things, Colin. And you've got to believe in people."

"I do. That doesn't have anything to do with it."

"Yes, it does. If you're like Toby, and believe the worst about everybody, then you're no better than the person that did this."

"Who said I'm like Toby? He's the way he is because his old man cheats and he's fat and he hates the world, and I feel sorry for him. But that doesn't mean I have to close my eyes to everything that happens."

"Well, let's just not talk about Toby, okay?"

"Okay."

Then I understood. It was my mentioning Toby's father's infidelities.

"Look," I said, changing the subject, "You ever heard of somebody called Drood?"

Stan shifted on the bed, pulling up a sock. "I think that's the family that owns Windsong. Why?"

I told him about our going up on the levee and how Sikes had caught us, and threatened us with Drood.

"That goddamned Toby," Stan said.

"Yeah."

A car door slammed in the driveway and a few minutes later Benson Chandler stuck his head in the door.

"Hi, guys. What's happening?"

"Just talking," Stan said, looking away.

"Your mom inside?" Dr. Chandler asked.

"Far as I know," Stan said.

"You men take it easy," Chandler said, smiling, and disappeared toward the back of the main house.

"He's home early," I said.

"He probably brought Mom a present," Stan said.

There was an awkward silence. Finally I said:

"I guess we won't be going back out there until they catch whoever did it."

"No. And they may not ever catch him."

"You don't think so? If it was Sikes . . ."

"It wasn't fucking Sikes, I told you."

"Okay, whoever. But . . ."

The slam of another car door, followed by a second door shutting, brought me up short.

"Now who the fuck's out there?" Stan muttered. "If that goddamned Toby came here . . ."

I followed him through the door and into the yard. He walked up the drive and then stopped short.

"Shit," he muttered.

"What?"

"Cops," he said, nodding at the plain white Ford parked behind his father's car.

"Cops?"

"Yes, damn it, look at the antenna."

"Oh, crap." I thought of Toby's bravado at cursing Sikes as we left. Even Sikes could get a license number . . .

"You think they already picked up Toby?" I whispered.

Stan shrugged. "I don't know. I wouldn't put it past that shit to throw the blame on you or Blaize, or even me."

A chill froze through my bones. I knew what he was saying was true.

"What should I do?" I asked.

"Take off. If they ask, I'll say I haven't seen you. Maybe they'll give up if they don't find you right away."

"Stan . . ."

"Get the hell out of here."

"But they'll go to my house."

"Only if they don't have anything else to do. But something else might happen between now and then. Now take off."

I knew he was right. There was no telling what Sikes had said and whatever Toby might have said would only have made it worse. I could see it right now: Toby, chagrined because I hadn't wanted to go home from school with him, might have claimed I was the one who'd yelled. And what if I'd dropped something along the road that night?

I felt my safe little world starting to slip away.

Five seconds later I was over his back fence and into the bamboo patch on the other side. I wandered the streets for hours, until well after dark. I knew my father would be worried, but what could I do? Finally, as I was walking down Cloverdale, a mile away from where either of us lived, a yellow Chrysler pulled up beside me and, through the open passenger-side window, I heard a familiar voice and saw a flash of garish jewelry.

"Colin, is that you?" It was Blanche St. Martin. I kept walking. Maybe she'd decide she'd made a mistake.

"Colin, you stop when I speak to you."

I halted, miserable. The door opened. "Get yourself in here. Your father is worried sick. He's called everywhere looking for you. He thought you'd been murdered or run over by a train."

"I was just walking," I said.

"Well, you get in here. I'm taking you home this minute. Your poor father."

I climbed in like a sheep on the way to slaughter, wishing the cloying perfume that filled the car were a poison gas that would end my suffering once and for all.

"Blaize is worried about you, too, you know. When he heard everybody was looking for you he almost had an asthma attack. It's really very thoughtless, Colin, to do that to your friends."

I tried to make myself smaller in the seat. But at least she hadn't said anything about the police.

My father opened the door on the third knock.

"He was down on Cloverdale," my captor pronounced. "I'll leave you to find out what he was doing there."

"Thank you, Blanche. I'll take care of it." My father shut the door behind her and shook his head.

"What the hell, Colin? You don't know how to use a telephone?"

"I'm sorry," I managed. "I didn't mean to worry anybody."

"Oh, hell, I knew you were all right. But I had to call around, and by the time Blanche St. Martin was finished, you were as good as dead."

"Dad . . ."

"Yes?"

I licked my lips, trying to screw up my courage. "Have the police . . . ?"

"What? Been looking for you? No, I was going to hold off calling them unless you stayed out all night. But I figured you'd be home. I remember how it was to be your age. You have a fight with one of your friends? Or were you going to see some girl I don't know about?"

"Dad . . ."

"Hey, you're fifteen. Pretty soon you'll be dating and then you'll be driving. No need to hurry things, but I expect you're normal in that respect. There are some pretty nice-looking young ladies in your class."

"I don't care about any of them," I said. "They're stupid. Most of them haven't ever read a book and those that have look like Ella Pitre."

"Ella's a nice girl," he said. "She just hasn't been gifted with the looks some of them have, and maybe that's not all bad. But, mark my words, one of these days a girl will come along and then everything will be different, overnight. Trust me."

I couldn't resist: "Is that how it was with you and Mom?"

He rubbed his jaw and headed toward the kitchen.

"Well, it wasn't that simple. At first we didn't hit it off. I was dating another girl, Corrine Dupuy. She was the first real girlfriend I ever had, unless you count puppy love in high school."

"I always thought Mom was your first girl."

He just smiled and took some plates out of the refrigerator. "She was my second girl, Corrine was the first. I was really in love with Corrine."

I felt embarrassment at the revelation, as if I were about to be told I was illegitimate.

"She was the first girl I met when I came down here from up north. She was a beautiful woman, the kind of girl all the boys want to date. I felt like I was the luckiest graduate student at LSU."

Corrine Dupuy. I'd never even heard the name before. Now I was being told I might have been her son instead of my real mother's.

"What happened?" I heard myself croak.

"Oh, your mother happened." He chuckled and put one of the dishes on the stove and turned on the gas burner. "She was friends with Corrine. Except not really; I think Corrine just brought her along to show she could have whoever she wanted. Corrine was a show-off."

He turned around from the stove to face me.

"Your mom told me later she didn't want to go, that Corrine dragged her along."

"It was a date?"

"More or less. I'd asked Corrine to go to the Paramount Theater and when I went to pick her up she asked if your mother could come, so what could I say?"

"You didn't want her along?"

"I guess I should've been happy to have two girls, but from the first time we met, your mom and I decided we didn't like each other."

"What?"

"That's right. She told me later she thought I was aloof, that I thought I was better than other people. I thought she was hard to get along with. She argued with everything I said."

"But how . . . ?"

"How did we ever get together?" He wandered over to the cabinet and took out the supper plates. "I guess because it was love at first sight after all."

"What?" I wrinkled my nose.

"Son, when a man and woman don't care about each other at all, they don't have any reason to fight. It's when they start out fighting all the time that there's something between them. They just don't want to admit it. In our case, your mom didn't want to admit she could be so attracted to a Yankee, who had such different ideas from hers. In my case, I guess I saw something underneath that intrigued me and I was frustrated at first that I couldn't figure out what it was."

"What happened to Corrine Dupuy?"

"Oh, she finally saw which way the wind was blowing. She surely didn't need me. She was in plenty of demand. She married an oil company man and they moved to Beaumont. He was killed in the war and I heard she remarried right afterward. Corrine could take care of herself."

I tried to absorb the thought: if he'd married Corrine Dupuy, my mother would still be alive. But, then, I wouldn't be who I was, so maybe it was a foolish speculation.

"Was she prettier than Mom?"

"She was more glamorous. But not more beautiful. Your mother was the most beautiful woman I ever met or ever will."

He paused, then gave me a strange look: "Do you remember her very well, Colin?"

"Sure."

He put a hand on my shoulder. "That's good. I'd hate for you to ever forget her. I think about her every day. Do you know, we were married twelve years, right after the war started and I was about to be shipped out, so we were apart three of those years. But the years we were together, we never had a fight, not even an argument."

I stared at him open-mouthed. How could he say that? I remembered that day like it was yesterday, the look on her face when she saw the car, her running back into the house, the slamming door . . . or was it that he didn't want to remember it?

After supper I wanted to call Stan, but I was afraid. What if he told me the cops really were looking for me? But that was crazy: If they were looking for me, they'd have been here by now. I decided I'd wait and ask him tomorrow at school. That was plenty soon enough.

CHAPTER ELEVEN

I leave the old house where I used to live, knowing if I stay here much longer someone will call the police to report a suspicious character. And maybe I am a suspicious character, for what will I say if a policeman pulls up beside me, asks why I am here?

"I'm looking into a murder, Officer. Only it happened before you were born."

When you are young you take your situation for granted. I missed my mother, but somehow I figured that this was the way things were supposed to be, and it was only much later that I realized how much grief I had repressed. I think it was because my father so seldom let himself show emotion, saving it all for the poems he wrote. He was always still up when I went to bed and there were times when I got up in the middle of the night for water or to go to the bathroom, and the light in the breakfast room was on, and when I peeked in, I would see him, bent over his yellow notepad, pencil in hand. Once, when the sound of my footsteps startled him, his head whipped around and I thought for a moment that he didn't recognize me and for the barest moment I was afraid, as if I had come upon a stranger in the act of burglary.

Years after his death, his second wife, Stella, sent me a cardboard box with stacks of papers inside. Her note said simply:

Colin, your father wrote these before he met me, and they seem to have to do with your mother. I think it best that you have them.

I held the box, hands trembling, unsure whether I dared open it. My parents were dead and there was nothing these papers could do to bring them back. If I opened the box and read what was inside, it would be like unsealing their coffins and peering at their long-dead faces.

I put the box on a shelf and never opened it. Maybe, I thought, the time would come, but not then.

• • •

The next day at school I tried to ask Stan what the cops had wanted, but he jerked away, mumbling something I couldn't understand. I watched him melt into the crowd changing classes, stunned.

What had I done? Why was he angry with me, and for what?

At lunchtime I didn't see him in the cafeteria and Blaize sidled up to me, placing his tray on the table beside mine.

"Is it true about Stan?" he asked, keeping his voice low.

"What?"

"His mom came and got him before the bell rang."

"Why?"

He leaned closer to me and I saw several heads turn our way.

"Toby says the cops went to his house yesterday and searched it. He says they found all kinds of letters and things that showed his old man and Senorita Gloria were making out."

I felt a sinking sensation. Now I understood about the fight on the lawn and I understood about the unmarked car that had pulled into the driveway right after Stan's father got home.

"Are you sure?"

"It must be. I mean, Toby said they have his old man down-town right now, questioning him. He says when they searched through her things they found some letters he sent her."

"Jesus." I recalled Stan's adamant defense of the Spanish teacher.

"I didn't know they even knew each other," I said.

"My mom says he was popular. He's a woman's doctor, you know. She says some of those women's doctors go into it so they can get women to take off their clothes."

"Yeah, but was she his patient?"

"That's what I heard. I heard she went to him for female problems."

"Who's saying that?"

"Lots of people. Everybody's talking about it."

"Well, do you believe it?" I asked. "I mean, that they were having it on?"

He shrugged. "I think it's possible."

"Because Toby said so?"

"No. It's just . . ."

"What?"

"Well, I watched her in class. She used to, well, like flirt with some of the guys, her students. Always patting them and hug-ging. She used to say that's the way people were where she came from, but I don't know."

I thought of the day I'd run into her in the hallway.

"That doesn't mean he killed her," I said. "I mean, if she was that way, she may have been screwing a lot of guys. Any one of 'em could've done it."

"Yeah," Blaize said but he didn't sound convinced.

• • •

The next day there was a memorial service for the murdered teacher at the Catholic Chapel on campus, and the student body was excused to attend. Her body had been shipped back to South Texas, so there was no coffin, just some flowers and a brief eulogy by the priest and a somewhat longer one by Dr. Cornwall, who talked about how he hadn't been privileged to know her for very long but it had been a pleasure to work with her, because she was so well-liked and easy to get along with. He said none of us could fathom why these things happened, and managed to work in again that he hadn't known her for long, or knew anything about her personal life, because his relationship with her had been purely professional, but he said she'd be missed and that it was a dark day for education and for the school itself and for every student. Finally, he told us that as great as the evil was that had happened to Senorita Gloria, it was just as bad to spread rumors and gossip, and that he knew there'd been all kinds of talk, and such talk could be very hurtful to innocent people, and he said he had full faith in the police and the district attorney and that we should all just mind our business and let them do what they were trained to do.

That night my father got another phone call, this one from somebody in his department. His face turned grave and when he hung up the phone he came to where I was watching TV, trying to calculate whether I should call Stan or not, and turned the set off.

My head jerked up because he only did that when he had something truly momentous to impart. He sat down beside me on the couch, taking care to pull up his pant legs.

"Now Colin," he said, "I don't want you to get too upset by what I'm going to tell you, but I think it's best you heard it from me."

I waited, afraid.

"I just got a call from Peter DeGarmo. He says the police have arrested Dr. Chandler."

He reached over and patted my shoulder. "I know how hard this is for you. You and Stan are close. And I know how hard it must be on Stanley. There've been all kinds of rumors flying around, and now this. I feel very sorry for him."

"But his dad didn't do it."

"We'd like to think that. It's certainly what *I* want to believe." He ran a hand though his short brown hair. "But I might as well tell you before you get it from somewhere else, in case you haven't already—it looks a lot like there was something going on between Miss Santana and Dr. Chandler, and that's what the police are looking at."

I didn't say anything. There was no sense confirming that the news was all over school.

He put his hand on my knee. "You know, son, sometimes grownups do things they wish they hadn't. Stupid, foolish things, on the spur of the moment. Some people are weak and some people crave excitement and some people get bored with their lives. Then they slip. Nobody's perfect, not you, not me, not Dr. Chandler. If he slipped, well, that's between him and his conscience and his family. What I'm saying is doing a foolish thing doesn't make him a murderer."

"But you think the thing between him and Senorita Gloria is true."

He sighed. "I don't want to think so, but it seems like there's evidence it is. The police wouldn't have arrested him if they didn't have something concrete."

"But what does that prove?"

"They'll say it shows he had motive. They'll say she tried to get him to leave his wife and threatened to expose him, or that they had a fight because she resisted his advances, or that he wanted her to marry him and she wouldn't. I don't know if there's anything to any of that. I hope and pray there isn't, for his and his family's sake. But as Stanley's friend you need to be prepared for what you're going to hear in the next few days and weeks. I'm afraid it's going to get very ugly."

I shut my eyes for a long minute, wishing it would all go away. He gave my knee a pat.

"Of course, he's hired a good lawyer. J. Carter Criswell. You can bet he'll pick apart every bit of evidence they try to use."

J. Carter Criswell, I thought: His son, J. Carter III, was a senior on the high school football team and a first class asshole.

"After all, so far it's just circumstantial," my father went on. "They don't have a witness. Nobody saw the two of them together at the cemetery. I guess, in fact, you and Stan are the closest to witnesses they have, because you saw the car driving away."

"God . . ."

He nodded. "They'll probably talk to you again, but when they do, I'll be there, and all you have to do is tell the truth. It was night, you didn't get a good look at the car, and that was that. You tell the truth and you'll always be okay."

The truth. What would he say if he knew the truth was that I was the last person to see Gloria Santana alive? Guilt weighed me down, but then I told myself, why should I feel guilty? I wasn't holding back anything that mattered. I hadn't seen the killer, just a dying woman. What difference to the case could that make?

Unless they somehow found out. Because Stan knew I'd gone down the road alone. He'd been asleep when I returned, and so he had no way of knowing I'd seen the dying woman, but if he mentioned my little excursion, what could I say to defend myself? I remembered Father O'Dwyer saying once in his sermon that only the guilty hold back the truth. And if anybody could ferret out the truth, it was J. Carter Criswell, the man who'd gotten off more murderers and crooked politicians than anybody else in the state.

• • •

It was Blaize who said we had to do something to prove Stan's father was innocent. I was seated at the end of a table in the lunchroom. Usually I ate with Stan, but he hadn't come to school again today and Blaize came up with his tray, looking unusually pale and set his food down beside my own.

"It's for Stan's sake," he said. "I mean, he's our friend."

I hadn't told anybody about the argument I'd witnessed between the Chandlers.

"I don't know what we can do that his lawyer isn't doing," I said. "Besides, how do we know he *didn't* do it?"

"You don't understand." Blaize's face was thin and earnest. "It's all over school now."

"Oh, shit," I said. "Well, we know Stan didn't do it."

"You know it and I believe you, but there are some saying maybe you're lying for him, or maybe he snuck away in the night . . ."

"Bastards. I bet it's Jennifer Broussard and that bunch." Jennifer went out with Fred Picou, who was a year older than we were and was a star pitcher on the baseball team.

I set down my forkful of macaroni and cheese, no longer hungry.

"Let 'em talk," I said.

"Colin, look: You don't know what it was like at those other schools. I didn't have any friends. I was always sick and when I wasn't sick I was practicing my piano. Do you know what's it's like to always be called queer because you don't go out for sports and you like music? When I came here I thought it would be the same way, but you and Stan, well, you treated me like a person. I'd feel the same way if it was you."

"Yeah, you're right. But the only thing we can do is find somebody else. Isn't that what Perry Mason does on TV all the time?"

"I'm serious, Colin. I don't mean just find somebody, I mean find the guilty one. Unless you think Stan or his dad did it."

"No, I don't think he did," I said, but it must have sounded weak, because he fixed me with his brooding eyes.

"Tell me, then: Say 'I don't think anybody in Stan Chandler's family had anything to do with the murder of Senorita Gloria.'"

"Oh, come on."

"No, damn it, say it."

I shrugged. "Okay, I don't think anybody in Stan's family had anything to do with the killing, all right?"

He relaxed slightly. "Okay."

"Then who does that leave? Sikes?"

He shook his head. "I don't think it was Sikes."

"Why? He's a mean son-of-a-bitch."

"We don't know that," Blaize pointed out. "All we've got is a bunch of stories from Toby."

"Bullshit. Old man Bergeron says it and, besides, you were in the car when he came after us the other day. We know he served time for knifing a man."

"That's just it. There are stories, but that's all. Don't you think if a bunch of women were missing it would be news?"

"Not if they were nigger women."

"I don't believe that. At some point something would have to be done. And if he knifed a man, it was in a fight, it wasn't sneaking up on anybody, at least that's what you told me Bergeron said."

"Okay, but what about the other day? You heard what the bastard said yourself."

"I heard him threaten us, but we were where we shouldn't have been. And he didn't really *do* anything."

"Well, you believe what you want. But I was there. Besides, who else is left besides some tramp?"

Blaize leaned close until his face was only inches from my own.

"You remember the man Sikes told us about, Drood?"

"Yeah. But who the hell is he?"

"I asked my mother. She knows about the old families around here. The Droods owned Windsong since right after the Civil War. The first Drood was a carpetbagger, came down from the north and bought it at a sheriff's auction, and they say he had all kinds of Negro mistresses and that his wife committed suicide, drowned herself in the river."

"So? That was a hundred fucking years ago."

"Let me finish. They said old man Drood went crazy after his wife drowned, used to ride through the fields at night on a black horse, kidnapping the slave women out of their houses and raping them, and then burying them alive near the old graveyard."

"It was after the Civil fucking War. There weren't any more slaves."

"You know what I mean: They weren't slaves but they had to work for him because they didn't have anywhere else to go." His eyes were as big as plates now, and seemed to burn with ancient fires. "Then, one night, when they were setting fire to the fields, he dragged off this one woman, and she ran away, right into the burning field, and he went after her, on his horse, wearing one of these long white coats they called dusters, and it caught fire, and the last anybody saw was him riding through the fire, all lit up like a Christmas tree, trailing flame and smoke. They said he disappeared back into the swamp and after that the darkies wouldn't go back there, because they always said the swamp was haunted by Massa Drood's ghost."

I snorted. "Where did you get that bullshit?"

"My mother," he said quietly. "And then, when I was sick the other day, I asked our maid, Lucretia, and she knew all about it, because her people came from the plantation next door."

"So you think old Sikes was threatening us with somebody that's been dead for a hundred years, or was he just threatening us with his ghost?"

"Will you listen, Colin? I'm trying to tell you: The Droods were all crazy, starting with that first one and, for all I know, they were crazy in the north, before that, but all we know is about when they came down south after the war. But this Drood had a son, and there was something wrong with him, too. My mother said the story was that Drood's wife was pregnant at the same time this Negro woman was, but that the white baby died so they put the Negro woman's baby in Drood's wife's arms, but when she saw he was dark-skinned, that was when she went and drowned herself."

It sounded suspiciously like a Bible story I'd heard in Catechism class, but I couldn't remember which story it was, because as Catholics we didn't learn much about the Old Testament.

"Anyhow," Blaize went on, excited, "this mulatto boy was raised as Drood's son, but before old Drood went crazy and burned himself up, he sent the boy up north to be raised by his folks up there, and the boy didn't come back for twenty years."

"So we're talking about what? Eighteen-ninety or something?"

"That's not the point. The point is that every Drood has been crazy ever since and they always send the boys up north to be educated, and then they come back here. And when they get back, they're as crazy as ever and all kinds of things happen. In the nineteen-twenties there was a murder of a professor on the campus, with an ax, and Lucretia said the cops knew it was a Drood who did it, but they couldn't prove it, on account of the Droods have a lot of money and can always buy out of it."

"That's what Lucretia says, huh?"

"Don't laugh. She knew all about it, and she said something else, too."

"Oh?

"She said the Sikes have been working for the Droods ever since the first Drood came down here. She said Sikes is a mean

white man—that's what she called him—but she said he just had
one aim, like all the Sikes before him, and that was to take care
of the Droods, even to take the blame for 'em if they have to."

"The blame?" I regarded the chocolate pudding in my spoon
and then decided I didn't want it.

"That's right. It was something about how the first Drood
saved the first Sikes in the Civil War, at Gettysburg, I think,
and ever since then the Sikes' have looked out for the Droods,
even if it meant going to jail for 'em or running the place while
the Droods were away. It's sort of like that high priest in the
Mummy, you know, the one who guards Kharis and . . ."

"And feeds him fucking tanna leaves. I guess Lucretia told
you that, too."

"No. And you don't have to believe all of it. I mean, maybe
Lucretia's full of it, but there's some truth there, because I
asked my mom, and she knew all about the Droods. At least,
she knows they're crazy, and she knows about the one Sikes was
talking about."

"Yeah?"

"She says the Droods almost lost everything in the Depres-
sion and old man Drood killed himself. His wife took their son
and went up north and nobody knew what happened, but a year
or so ago, the young Drood—Darwin his name was—showed
up again and took to living on the old place, by himself."

"Your mother says that?"

"Yes. And she knows about these old families."

There was no denying that.

I was still mulling over the possibility when Toby plopped
down beside me, his tray full of what most of us considered
inedible.

"You girls on a date?" he asked. "Or can I join you."

Nobody else wanted to sit with him, and we were almost finished, so I shrugged:

Toby forked a mountain of macaroni into his mouth, not bothering to wipe away the cheese that stuck to his lips.

"Still trying to decide who did it?" he asked.

"None of your business."

"You may change your tune when you hear what I know."

"You don't know shit," I said.

"No? I know about the lie detector test."

"What lie detector test?" Blaize asked.

Toby smacked his lips and forked in another load of maca-roni. He eyed Blaize's pudding. "Hey, you gonna eat that?"

"I don't know. What about the lie detector test?"

Toby helped himself to the pudding and I lowered my eyes as he filled his mouth.

"Well?" Blaize demanded.

"Well, what?" Toby asked, mouth still half full.

"Finish chewing," I said, disgusted.

"Screw you," Toby said and belched.

He eyed both our plates for anything we'd missed and then wiped his mouth with a hand.

"Okay, girls, here's the way it is, the latest from the court-house: Stan's old man agreed to a lie detector test and how do you think it came out?"

"How the fuck should we know?" I asked.

"Well, you think he did it, don't you?"

"I never said that," I told him.

"Look, either say what you're gonna say or shut up," Blaize said.

"Okay." Toby cocked his head and considered another group of students at the next table. "Look at 'em: gossip, gossip, gossip. Bunch of dumb assholes." He turned back to us: "Okay, here it is: The results of the test were inconclusive."

"Inconclusive?" Blaize and I said in unison.

"Do I stutter? There was no conclusive result, one way or the other."

"What does that mean?" Blaize asked.

Toby looked pained. "It means, dumbass, that Dr. Benson Chandler was too smart for 'em. He told the truth about some things and he huffed and puffed and tensed up on other questions that he gave truthful answers to. So they couldn't figure out what they call a baseline. That's what my old man said."

"You mean it was deliberate?" I asked.

"Christ yes. He's a doctor. He knows how to fuck up one of those machines."

"So they're going to let him go?" I asked.

"Shit, no. He claimed he was at a medical conference in Dallas, but the airline says he never took that plane, and he never registered. There's no proof he ever parked his car at the airport, like no parking receipt. So he could've just stayed so he and Gloria hot pants could get it on."

"That's still just circumstantial," I said. "I mean, nobody saw him with her, did they?"

"They're checking all that. But they're checking something else, too. I heard my old man telling my old lady."

"What?"

"Well, what if Chandler was screwing Gloria and his old lady found out about it? What if she was the one who did it? There's motive, see, and that's what cops look at. The triangle, it's called."

"That's crap," Blaize mumbled.

"How do you know, fairy boy? You mean if your old man was fucking your teacher your old lady wouldn't be pissed enough to kill her?"

Blaize's face flushed and he jumped up, almost upsetting his tray: "You shut up about my mother," he cried.

"Hey, it's just an example," Toby said. "Could've been Stan's older brother, Ben."

"And I guess you're going to spread this all over school," I said, disgusted.

"Don't have to. What do you think they're talking about over there? Won't be but another day before they hear it. Shit, man, this town is like a fucking auditorium. Everybody hears everything. I heard from my old man that the campus police chief got chewed out by the sheriff for talking to the dean. And you know the dean told old Cornhole."

That much was true; my father had often commented on how anything that happened at or near the university was known by everybody within a few hours.

. . .

That night I asked my father about the Droods.

He sighed and put down his paper.

"I guess everybody's fair game in this business." He sighed and picked up his pipe. "Well, I don't know much about them, son. Your mom, if she were alive, would know more, because she came from here. And your Uncle Royce could tell you a lot more. But as far as I know, the family's just about died out, except for young Darwin."

"Darwin?"

"The son. They sent him north for his education, to one of those exclusive prep schools, Exeter or Andover or Choate. Then he went on to one of the Ivy league colleges." He started to pack his pipe. "I think there was something peculiar about the boy. I'm not sure what. He had a nervous breakdown or something when he was about your age, home for the summer. I really don't remember because it was a while back, and folks like the Droods cover their tracks."

"I heard he came back."

"Did he? Well, then, he's got a lot of work to do, because after his folks died the place went to ruin."

"Do you think he's dangerous?"

My father frowned and put down his pipe. "Why would you ask that? Oh, I see: you're wondering if he might have killed your teacher."

"She wasn't my teacher."

"You know what I mean. Well, who can say what anybody else might do? All I can say is that just because somebody has a nervous breakdown doesn't mean he's a killer."

"But do you think Stan's dad's the killer, then? Or his mom? Or . . ."

"Son, I don't know what to believe. All I know is that all this speculation can't do anybody any good. The authorities are investigating. That's their job, and they do it better than you or I, so why don't we leave it to them?"

I started to tell him about the results of the lie detector test, then held back. Maybe he knew but, then again, maybe he didn't. Whatever the case, it was clear he didn't know anything more than I did at this point.

CHAPTER TWELVE

I awaken and shower, feeling empty. The memories of those days have flooded back like flotsam propelled by raging waters.

Maybe it is time to go back to the River Road. Isn't that why I've come? Do I intend to stay in the hotel room and never summon the courage to do what I came here to do?

But it will be so much easier if I can enjoy some support, validate the memories by exposing them to someone who was there and will know what is true and what my mind may have invented.

I look at my watch: It is six-thirty. Blaize probably hasn't yet left for school.

Hand trembling, I lift the phone and punch in his number.

"I'm sorry to call so early," I say when he answers.

When he speaks, there is resignation in his voice: "I knew you'd call back. I've been waiting."

"I'm sorry."

"I'll get away for lunch. Do you know where Baton Rouge High is?"

"I think I remember."

"There's a shopping center almost across the street, in Westmoreland, with a Piccadilly Cafeteria. I'll meet you there at noon."

I drive and reach the school half an hour early. It is as I remember it, a three-story Gothic structure built in the mid-twenties. It has been converted into a Magnet school, a haven for the more promising students, in an attempt to slow white flight. I park on a side street, near a tattoo parlor, and watch the students lying on the big grassy lawn, under the live oaks. Some of the girls have pink hair and, though I cannot get close enough to see, I am sure they wear body jewelry and are pierced in places that would have been unthinkable forty years ago.

I am hardly surprised, because that is the way it is in Colorado, too. Maybe I'm just surprised that it has reached this town, which, as part of the South, has always been at the end of social change.

I leave the side street and find a place in the parking lot in front of a row of shops that range from a kidney dialysis unit to a dollar store. In the center of the block is the cafeteria.

It is noon now and people are trickling in. All at once I wonder how I will know Blaize St. Martin. It has been so long . . . But then I see him walking diagonally across the lot, a tall, graying man with glasses, though not with the unhealthy pallor I recall from high school. I get out and we shake hands.

"It's good to see you," I say, and he gives me a shy smile.

"A long time, Colin," is all he says.

We go inside, passing down the line to order, and I catch myself smiling at the hot dishes: the heapings of red beans and rice, the crawfish etouffé, the cornbread that I remember from my youth.

"Not exactly the school cafeteria," I say.

"Not exactly," Blaize says, returning my smile. I look for clues that will tell me about his present life but there's nothing, no wedding ring, no necklace that might hold a religious medal or a peace symbol.

We carry our trays to a booth in a corner, against the wall, and I reflect that in the old days, when my father and I came here to eat after church, there were always white-coated waiters who performed this service, and my father always gave me a dime to tip them with.

"You have a son," I say, as we settle in.

He nods, lifting his iced tea. "His mother and I divorced years ago."

I make an appropriate noise.

"Here." He produces a photograph from his wallet and I see a handsome, dark young man with the same brooding eyes as his father. "We don't see each other much."

I nod. I know the havoc that divorce can wreak, from what has happened in the lives of other friends.

"I guess you have children, too," he says, picking up a piece of cornbread.

I show him my pictures of Colin, Jr., and Caitlin, whom we call Honey.

"And this is Carolyn," I say. The picture is twenty-five years old, before there was any gray in her hair, but it is the one I have always loved.

"How's your mother?" I ask, assuming she has died long ago, but he surprises me:

"She's in an assisted-care place. She doesn't remember things very well these days. I had her with me for a long time, but I couldn't be there to watch her and . . ."

"I understand."

Blaize plays with his glass, turning it around slowly, nervous.

I bring up the dreams again and he looks down at the polished surface of the table.

"I used to have them, too," he says. "But not for a long time."

Now I understand his reluctance: he is afraid I will stir up what may be only slumbering.

His head jerks up then and he stares at me with the same burning eyes I remember:

"Colin, coming back here wasn't a good idea. It isn't going to do you any good. Believe me, it'll only make things worse." He leans forward. "It took me forever. I had a nervous breakdown. That's what they used to call 'em. The fact is I got depressed and I saw it all happening again, whenever I went to bed. It got to where I was scared to close my eyes. My mother must have paid thousands to shrinks but do you know the only good advice I got? Get away for a while. Give myself and everybody else a chance to forget. So I did. I traveled for a year or so, went to the Coast, to New York, and the only reason I came back was because she got sick. I met this girl and got married and one night I woke up and realized I hadn't had one of the dreams. After a while it got so I almost never had them. Not even when my marriage broke up. But you know what? In all that time I stayed away."

"Stayed away?"

"From the levee." He takes a deep breath. "I never went back there. The closest I ever got was once when some friends I was with took a ride down the River Road. I closed my eyes until we were past the place. When they asked why, I told them I was car sick." His smile is weak, like sunshine beaten back by storm clouds. "I guess that makes me a coward. But you know what? I don't care."

We eat in silence, two strangers who have nothing further to say to each other, but when we finish I know I can't let it go. I've come too far.

"I'm going to go try to find the old camping spot," I say.

He shakes his head, wadding his napkin.

"It won't be there. They've fenced the whole levee and the Corps of Engineers has put concrete matting on the batture. But the camp spot fell into the river a long time before that. And I'm glad it did." The burning eyes again: "What we did was wrong, Colin. Please don't rake it up."

I watch him walk away, his body a little less dense, it seems, than when he came in, as if by merely discussing the past he has lost some atoms, started to fade away into that imaginary time of memory.

. . .

I can't put my finger on when we began to distance ourselves from Stan. Maybe it was just the end of school and the fact that we no longer saw each other every day. Or maybe it was because on the last day of school when I tried to talk to him the words fumbled out like a loose football and I said something about how everything would be all right and he just looked at me as if he didn't understand and walked away. Or maybe it was the stories everybody was hearing now about his father's affairs.

My own father must have noticed my moroseness and perhaps that's why he let me take the driver's test in early June. I'd taken the required Driver's Ed in school that year and most of the others my age were already driving. I passed on the first try and one sunny day walked away with a fresh driver's license and my father's admonition to be careful ringing in my ears.

I dropped him at his office, for he was teaching summer school, and drove around town for a while, wondering which of my friends to surprise. I went past Blaize's apartment, but I remembered that his mother had taken him on a short trip to the Gulf Coast, to visit relatives. I thought of Toby, but he'd demand that I prove how fast I could go and I didn't need a speeding ticket my first day. I even eased past Stan's house, slow as a sigh, but when I saw that, while Mrs. Chandler's car was gone, his father's car was in the drive, I kept going. Stan might be in his little house to the rear. Or he might be with his mother. But to find out, I'd have to see his father, and what was I going to do, smile and ask how business was? Then it came to me how odd it was that at one in the afternoon, on what should have been a workday, a doctor should be at home. Did that mean his partners at the clinic had laid him off? That he'd lost his medical license? That he was down at the police station right now being grilled?

Where I ended up was at Bergeron's store.

He was watching the little TV when I came in, some game show, and when he saw me alone he seemed surprised.

"Where's the friends?" he asked.

I shrugged. "Don't know. I'm just out driving."

He chuckled. "Driving, huh?"

"Yes, sir." I went to the cooler and drew out a Coke.

"Well, don't drive past Sikes' house. Little niggers threw rocks at his place again last night and he's raising hell. Already had the sheriffs out here once."

"I don't guess they found out any more about the murder."

"No, and they never will. It'll go down like all the rest of 'em. Unsolved, even if it was a white lady."

"Mr. Bergeron, who are the Droods?"

He rubbed a grizzled jaw.

"The Droods? Hell, they own Windsong, them." He shook his head. "They are a strange bunch of people, the Droods."

"How do you mean?"

He cleared his throat and moved down the counter, away from the noise of the little television.

"Don't get the wrong idea: I always got along with 'em. When I saw 'em, that is. But Gaston Drood was a strange man."

"Gaston Drood?"

"The father. See, when young Gaston was growing up, the place was going downhill. Not as bad as it is now, but still, they let the sugarhouse fall in and that meant they had to take their cane over to Ascension Parish to get milled. Bad business people, the Droods. But young Gaston managed to marry a rich girl, Annabelle Grayson. Put all her inheritance into the place. I remember that. I was a youngster then, your age. But they said Gaston only married her to get his hands on her money and when she figured that out she went crazy. But not before she had a son, young Darwin. When his momma got real bad, they sent him away to school up north. I don't guess it was more than a year after that—toward the end of the War, I think—they found her floating in the river."

It sounded almost play for play like what Blaize's maid had told him, only with the generations transposed and a few embellishments.

But Bergeron wasn't finished.

"Now there were rumors she tried to stab Gaston and he killed her in self-defense and then he threw her body in the river, but there was also a story that Sikes did it. He hadn't been there that long and if you ask me, well, she was a pretty woman and Gaston was gone a lot . . ."

"The police didn't investigate?"

"Boy, ain't you learned money talks? Besides, by the time her body washed up down near Donaldsonville, couldn't nobody tell how she was killed."

"Was that when Darwin Drood came back? I mean, the first time?"

"No. That wasn't until six, seven years ago. Fifty-two, I think it was. I never saw him. He left again pretty quick. I think him and his daddy didn't get along. Gaston was drunk most of the time by then. Boy went on back north and Gaston died the next year. Place ran down then worse than back before Gaston married Annabelle. Sikes was supposed to take care of it, but that *fils putain* . . ."

"He's back now, though, right?"

"That's right. But don't ask me why. If it's to fix the place up I haven't seen much difference. Man keeps to himself. I haven't seen him but once close up and he was nice enough, just shy, like he didn't want to talk. Sleeps in one of the outbuildings that he got Sikes to fix up. The big house ain't fit for nobody to live in."

"You don't think he killed her?" I asked.

The storekeeper made a face. "If he had anything to do with it, he put Sikes up to it. You mark my words, if they ever find out, it'll be Sikes they catch."

I finished my Dr. Pepper and set the bottle on the wooden counter.

"Look, don't be going over there," Bergeron called after me. "There's lights in the old house at night. Lights and sounds. Niggers think it's haunted."

"Do *you*, Mr. Bergeron?"

"I don't know about that, but it may be something almost as bad, like devil worship. Craziness runs in that family."

I left and drove slowly down the River Road, passing the line of tenant shacks that faced the levee. A lone black boy on a red bike did figure eights in the gravel and I wondered if he was one of those who had pelted Sikes' house with rocks. Somehow I felt a deep kinship with him and I almost thought I ought to stop and congratulate him for a job well done. But when our eyes met there was only blankness in his own, the kind I was used to, that told me he wasn't letting a white man see any deeper than the surface.

Ahead, visible across the shimmering fields, was the big house of Windsong, shadowed by pecans and oaks and I slowed. I wondered if Bergeron had been telling the truth about strange lights and sounds. Maybe he was just trying to scare us away, save us from getting into trouble with Sikes. But my mother had always described Cajuns as superstitious, as opposed to her own family, who'd come over from Alsace in the mid-1800s, and had always worked in middle-class professions.

And, besides, Bergeron had always played straight with us
before. I eased off the accelerator, let the car slow to a crawl and
tried to imagine the sounds. What were they? Shrieks? Moans?
Creakings? Bergeron hadn't characterized them, so there was
no way to say. And then I remembered that he hadn't claimed to
hear them himself—It was the Negroes who'd heard them and
everybody knew they were notoriously superstitious.

Then I eyed the outbuildings. One, closer to the big house than
the others, might have at one time been a commissary or school
building. Was that where Darwin Drood lived? I searched for a
vehicle but there was none. Did that mean young Drood didn't
drive? Or just that he wasn't there right now. The shutters of the
big house still hung askew and it didn't look as if anyone had
done anything to try to clean up or repair the place. Why hadn't
he fired Sikes for letting the place get so run down? Did Sikes have
something on him? Maybe young Drood was as much afraid of
Sikes as were all of the blacks who lived along the River Road.

I'd become so engrossed in my speculations that when I
looked up my front wheel was inches from the ditch and I jerked
the car back onto the gravel. Damn. That wouldn't be so good,
getting stuck and having to walk all the way back to the store to
get Bergeron to pull me out with his truck.

I kept my eyes on the road thereafter, checking Sikes' place
out of the corner of my eye.

His truck wasn't there and if the stone throwing of the night
before had done any damage, you couldn't tell from the general
disrepair of the place. I sped up then, spewing dust behind me,
and saw the little grove of trees in the center of the field. The
cemetery. Maybe if I drove up there, got out and looked around,
I could find something the cops had missed. They were through
with the place, anyway. It wasn't a crime scene any more. There
was no sign saying I couldn't go there. I turned in at the little
road and stopped.

All at once the hairs on the back of my neck started to prickle, as if someone—or something—were watching me. It was crazy, because it was mid-morning, the sun was bright in a cloudless sky, and in two hours the temperature would be in the nineties.

I turned and looked over my shoulder.

There was only a cow on the levee.

Then, as I watched, I realized it was no cow, but a horse and rider, at the top of the levee, where I'd left Stan that night. A lone rider, looking down at me.

I backed into the River Road without checking my mirror and then gunned the engine, heading back to town in a plume of dust.

• • •

The next morning I slip into the campus chapel for the early Mass. It is where my parents used to go, and from which my mother was buried, even though we officially belonged to St. Agnes Parish. But everything is different. The Mass is in English and the priest faces the people. There is a part of the Mass where everyone greets his neighbor. I vaguely remember when the reforms came in, as the result of good Pope John XXIII but by then I'd stopped going to church. My father had grumbled about the changes, saying that Mass had been made into a social event rather than a communication between man and God. I don't know why I came here this morning. I guess that I expected the incense smell and the sight of the flickering candles to evoke memories, to bore a tunnel through the dreams and reveal with the clarity of the beatific vision what happened after I left the cemetery that day.

Blaize was Catholic but I seldom saw him at Mass, because his mother was strict about remaining within their own parish.

Stan and his family were Episcopalian, and I'm not sure where they worshipped, but after morning Mass I go downtown to St. James, the ivy-covered, ancient brick church that is among the oldest in the city. There are no ghosts on the sidewalk.

• • •

The day after I drove to the cemetery Dr. Benson Chandler was indicted for the murder of Gloria Santana.

I was scheduled to attend enrichment classes during the summer session—a way of keeping me off the streets—but the session hadn't started yet and so for the next few days I was being left alone while my father went to his office, usually for half a day. So he wasn't there when the phone rang and I heard Toby triumphantly telling me the news:

"But the evidence . . ." I said.

"They've got the love letters he sent her," Toby said. "And they've got one he wrote her just the day before he killed her that threatened her ass."

"Threatened her?" I asked.

"Yeah. She was spreading it around and he was jealous. Said he wanted her to himself and he'd kill her and anybody else who tried to get in the way."

For a long time I was at a loss for words. Could it be true? I kept seeing her that day at school, when she'd bumped into me. I could believe she was hot-blooded, like everybody said Latins were, and that she was doing it with some guy, but with more than one?

"She was a teacher," I blurted.

"She has it in the same place," Toby said.

"Well, do they know who the other guy is? Why don't they arrest him?"

"They're investigating. Personally, I'd look at old Cornhole. But it doesn't matter, see: Chandler said he'd see her dead before anybody else had her."

"I still don't believe it," I said, though I knew it was only loyalty to Stan that was talking.

"You don't have to, pussy. Chandler doesn't have an alibi, and the neighbors said they always heard him and Stan's mom arguing. Seems like everybody in the whole fucking neighborhood knew they didn't get along. She even told one of her friends she was thinking about a divorce."

So what I'd seen hadn't been unusual after all. I remembered that morning, Stan sitting on the edge of the overhang, with the river below:

"You ever think about what it's like to be dead?"

"What?"

"To be dead. Not to exist."

Then the overhang had "accidentally" given way, only my reaching out had kept him from falling into the current.

Now I understood. He'd known about his parents and it was almost too much to bear . . .

"What does Dr. Chandler's lawyer say?" I asked Toby.

"Same as any lawyer. He says the doc is innocent and they'll wait till the trial to show what they've got."

"Have you seen Stan?" I asked.

"No. Hey, he's your asshole buddy, not mine."

"I was out there yesterday," I blurted.

"Where?"

"The cemetery."

"How the hell did you get there?"

"I drove."

"Bullshit. You wouldn't take your old man's car without telling him."

"He let me. I got my license the other day."

Silence, this time from his end, as he realized his days as a necessary means of transportation were over.

"And you know what?" I said before he could respond. "I'm going back out there now."

"What do you mean?"

"I mean maybe whoever did it left something the cops didn't find. Maybe if Senorita Gloria was screwing somebody else, they did it, and maybe they left something the cops didn't find."

"You're full of shit. The cops combed that whole area."

"You said your old man called the Sheriff's Department a bunch of trained monkeys, that a Boy Scout could do just as good."

"Yeah, well, they found everything there was to find out there."

"How do you know?"

"I just fucking do."

"And you're just fucking full of shit. You're scared to go out there and find out."

"What are you talking about?"

And before I could stop myself I was saying it:

"I'm going out there and I'm going to do my own damn search. Maybe I won't find anything, maybe it'll be a waste of time, but Stan's our friend and if somebody else did this, then the least any of us can do is try to find out."

"You're crazy as shit."

"Maybe so, but you're the one always saying the cops around here just grab the first person they can and stop looking after that."

"So you're just going to walk around out there in broad daylight, looking at the grass and under tombstones."

"No, fucker, I'm going to go out there tonight. I'm going to use a flashlight, okay?"

"You're so full of shit. Your old man ain't about to give you his car."

I took a deep breath: "My old man will be sleeping."

"You're lying."

"Am I? Come with me, then."

"Tonight?"

"Tonight. Unless you're just a sack of bullshit on legs."

"What time?"

"Make it one-thirty. I'll drive down your street, real slow. If you ain't outside waiting I'll know you're just a bullshitting asshole."

"Don't worry, you cunt, I'll be there."

And that's how it happened, something I'd never planned, but that just jumped out. Under any other circumstances I'd never have thought of taking my dad's car. But I kept thinking about Stan, sitting on that bluff, and the vacant look on his face, like he only wanted a way out. And if I didn't do *something*, no matter how futile, not only would I have to live with it for the rest of my life, but I'd have to put up with Toby's bullshit.

That night it was hot when I turned in. I lay in bed with the windows open and the table fan purring on the bookcase, five feet away, alternately washing me with currents of warm air. From the next room came the thrum of the window air conditioner, which my father had purchased last year, and I knew that with its noise he'd never hear me tiptoeing out down the hall or the sound of the car engine starting.

It was stupid, I told myself, and I lay on the sheets, sweating, for a long time. I could just close my eyes, forget about it, and let events take their course.

And listen to Toby's taunts tomorrow.

Did I really care what he thought or said? Wasn't Stan what it was about? Wasn't he my friend? And if I hadn't run away that night, wasn't there a chance she would have spoken aloud the name of the real killer before she died?

I slipped on my clothes and, shoes in hand, went to the brass hook where my father kept the keys.

CHAPTER THIRTEEN

Any hope that Toby wouldn't be there was dashed when I eased down his street and saw a figure disengage itself from the shadow of the crepe myrtle on his front lawn. He slid into the car quickly for all his girth, rolled down the window and lit up a cigarette.

"I thought you wouldn't show up," he said.

"Why wouldn't I?"

"I thought some of Blaize might of rubbed off on you."

"What's this with Blaize? He's weak, okay, 'cause he has asthma. That isn't his fault."

"He's a fairy."

"Shove it."

"Then why isn't he with us?"

"I didn't ask him."

"Because you know he's a fairy."

"Because I don't think he could get out of his place as easy as we can."

"That's the fucking-A truth, with that old lady of his. She's a loon case."

"That something else your old man told you?"

"Didn't have to—Just look at her, hovering over poor little boy Blaize, scared to death he's going to catch cold or the clap or something. That's what makes fairies."

"Who says?"

"Freud says."

"Fuck him."

Toby guffawed. "So what is it you expect us to find tonight?"

"Maybe nothing. But I figure if there's the slightest chance, we owe it to Stan."

"Yeah, well, what if it only confirms his old man's guilty?"

I hadn't thought about that one. "Well, what would that be? He sure as hell didn't drop his wallet."

"A rubber, dickless. They can get a blood type from the cum in a rubber."

"We'll take the chance."

"Yeah. Well, if it is a rubber, I'll let you handle it."

"Thanks."

"Suppose it's something that points to somebody else," Toby said, exhaling a cloud of smoke.

"That's what we want."

"But what if it points to somebody you don't want it to?"

"Like who?"

"Well, like Stan. I mean, what if he knew about his old man and Gloria and he got pissed at her for ruining the family?"

"Stan was with me, remember?"

"But you had to sleep. He could have gotten up when you guys were sleeping and gone down there."

"But we saw the car . . ."

"You saw a car. Who the fuck knows if that car had anything to do with the killing? That could've been somebody out screwing his girlfriend. The killing could have happened an hour later."

"It didn't, though," I said.

"How do you know?"

For a second the admission of what I'd seen hovered on my tongue, but I ended up just shaking my head.

"It just didn't. There's no way Stan would have known to get up in the middle of the night and go down there and just happen to catch his dad and Gloria Santana."

"Unless he knew beforehand. Unless it was all planned."

"That's a crock of shit."

"Okay." He flipped his glowing butt through the window. The campus was quiet as we crossed Nicholson and passed the looming baseball stadium. The levee was just ahead now, a low, black screen rising from the ground.

"Then maybe *you* did it," Toby said.

"You fucker. Maybe you did it. You're the one who left us out there. You weren't there all night."

Toby croaked out a laugh.

"I got a alibi, dickhead. I was with Michelle."

I felt something hit me in the belly. "Michelle Bergeron?"

"You know any other Michelle?"

"You're really a lying sack of crap."

"She gives a blow job like a vacuum cleaner. And her tits . . ."

"Jesus, you're a liar."

But Toby just chuckled. "You ought to try her sometime. If you can keep it up long enough."

We came to the gravel and I headed south.

"Or it could've been Stan's brother or his old lady," Toby said. "The doc could be protecting them."

"If you're so sure one of them did it, why the hell did you even come with me?"

"What the hell else do I have to do?"

We passed Bergeron's darkened store. The idea of Michelle Bergeron with a slob like Toby was ridiculous, but down deep there was a seed of doubt. Windsong was quiet, too, no lights or shrieks, nor was there any light at the Sikes place, though this time his pickup was in the front yard, next to the Belair on blocks.

We came to the cemetery road and I stopped.

"Well?" Toby asked. "Aren't you going to drive in?"

I was already thinking about how I could turn around quickly if I had to.

"I don't want to drive over any evidence."

"Shit, the cops have already gone up and down this road a couple hundred times."

He was right, of course, and there should be space at the cemetery to turn around.

I cut the headlights, leaving only the dimmers on, and we bounced slowly over the ruts, drawing ever closer to the spot where a dying woman had reached out, calling for my help.

"What's wrong?" Toby asked. "This ain't the graveyard, it's up there."

"I know where it is," I snapped. A few seconds later we came into a little clearing, peopled by luminous tombstones.

I started to turn around so I could leave in a hurry if I had to, but Toby was already getting out. "What the fuck are you doing?"

He flicked on his cigarette lighter and I gave up, sliding the gearshift lever into park and leaving the engine running. I picked up my flashlight and opened my door, my feet crushing the dry grass. Around us, fireflies blinked like winking eyes and in the ditch by the little road frogs croaked.

"Here's where it happened," Toby said, the flickering flame of his lighter giving his face an evil cast. "The cops figure she got out first and he got out after her. They don't know if they'd screwed already or not, but they were standing right about where you are now and they started to argue."

"You said she was raped."

"They thought she was, but they fucked up, okay? Now shut up and listen: she tried to run away and he grabbed her. He pulled out a pocket knife, probably brought it just for this, and he cut her right in the guts."

I started to tremble, felt my gorge rising.

"But that didn't kill her right off. She spurted blood all over him and then she turned around to run. He caught up with her and stabbed her in the back, six or eight times."

"Toby, for God's sake . . ."

"She went down to her knees and he grabbed her head then and cut her under the chin."

Amid the nausea a sudden thought came to me.

"Does that mean she couldn't have said anything after that?"

"I dunno. Why?"

"Just asking."

"Well, anyhow, she fell down, and then he rolled her over. They figure she was still alive, because there were cuts on her arms, like she was trying to protect herself."

It was as real as if I was seeing it happen, and the terrible thing was that the figure I saw bending over her really was Dr. Benson Chandler.

"Then he cut off her tits."

"What?"

"He cut off her tits. They found 'em in the grass."

"She had to be dead by then," I said. Maybe what I'd seen hadn't been the dying woman after all. Maybe it had been a figment of my imagination . . .

"He thought she was. He left, they figure. But she got up somehow and staggered a few feet down the road. That's where they found her."

My knees started to give out and I reached out to steady myself against a nearby cedar tree.

"What's wrong?"

"Nothing," I managed, trying to shove the apparition from my mind. I flipped on my flashlight and started to walk between the gravestones. Some were plain white slabs of concrete with no marking at all, and others had inscriptions that had been made while the cement was still wet. But most of the graves were unmarked, simple depressions in the ground whose wooden markers had long since rotted.

If there'd ever been anything here, the police had already found it, because the ground was bare of foreign objects, except for a couple of cigarette butts that could have been dropped by the detectives.

"Here's one died in 1915," Toby said. "That was the year my old man was born."

"Aren't you going to help?"

"Help what? I don't know what we're supposed to be looking for."

I moved away from the graves and onto the hard-packed dirt road, but Toby was right: the cop cars had obliterated anything that might have been here.

I went back to the cemetery and shined my light up at the tree fringe.

"What do you expect to find out there?" Toby asked, sitting down on one of the cement slabs.

"What if she threw something, like maybe she tore off his watch, or a ring or . . ."

"Sure."

But there were no glimmers in the trees and I flicked off the beam. What did that leave? I turned the light back on and by accident it hit the back fence, where a cluster of blackberry vines screened the cemetery from the adjacent pasture.

I walked over and shined the light in the thicket.

"You think they came out here to pick berries?" Toby asked.

"I think she could've run away and been stopped at the fence, couldn't she?" I asked.

"I told you how she was killed. It was over there, by your car."

"But you weren't here. Neither were the cops."

"They could tell by the blood on the grass."

"And they don't ever make mistakes."

He shrugged. "Just hurry up. It's getting cold out here."

I walked the fence line, knowing it was a waste of time, but knowing I had to do it.

And when I reached the corner post, the light hit something deep in the shadows of the thicket, sending a single gleam back at me.

I reached in slowly, knowing that snakes loved blackberry thickets, and that in all probability all I was going to find for my efforts would be a piece of tinfoil from chewing gum.

My fingers touched something hard, cold, closed around it.

I carefully drew the object out, ignoring the thorns.

I shined the light down on it.

It was a single gold earring with a dangling, five pointed star.

"Jesus," I said to myself.

"What?" Toby hoisted himself to his feet and lumbered over. I showed him the object.

"You found that in there?" he asked.

"Yeah. You think we're wasting our time now?"

"It could be anybody's. Some college girl's. Some nigger woman who came back here to clean the graves."

"I think it was *hers*," I said. "I think he tore it off her when they were struggling and it got thrown into the bushes."

"You gonna turn it in as evidence, then?"

"I don't know. I mean, like you say, it doesn't prove anything. Especially if it was hers."

"You ever see her wearing it?" he asked.

"I wasn't in her class. But Blaize was. I'll show it to him. He may remember."

"Yeah, sure," Toby said, disgusted. "Now you ready to go?"

I shook my head, clutching the earring in one hand.

"Yeah. I'm ready."

CHAPTER FOURTEEN

The next day I showed the earring to Blaize and the cops came looking for me.

I thought it was funny that Toby didn't say anything about wanting to be there when I showed Blaize. He just left the car as quickly as he could and vanished back into the shadows of his front yard, heading, no doubt, for his bedroom window. I went home, replaced the keys on the hook in the breakfast room, and lay down in my underwear, trying to will myself to sleep. But the same scenario kept running through my mind.

He was chasing her with the knife, they were struggling, she twisted, the knife slashed across her neck, she lurched out of his grip and he reached out for her and somehow caught her earring instead. It ripped loose, which must have hurt, since it was for a pierced ear. He threw the earring away and ran after her and the rest was probably the way Toby had described it.

Had she been able to scream or had her vocal cords been severed? Could she have told me his name if I hadn't acted the coward that night and run?

I drifted off some time around six, and woke up moments later to hear my father moving around the house, preparing to head out for the office. Half an hour later, when I heard the car motor start, I dressed, gobbled a bowl of raisin bran, and, bleary-eyed, stuck the earring deep into my pocket and headed for Blaize's apartment.

His mother greeted me at the door in her bathrobe.

"It's a little early, isn't it, Colin? Blaize is still asleep."

"I'm sorry." It hadn't occurred to me that at eight on a Friday morning people might still be in bed.

"That's perfectly all right. He just had a little episode last night. It's especially bad at this time of year, with the pollens."

I nodded, suddenly uncomfortable in her presence. Judging from her sunken cheeks, the black smudges under her eyes and the pallor of her complexion sans makeup, the night had been a hard one for both of them. The image clashed with the one I'd always had of Blanche St. Martin, the woman who was in total control.

"What if I have him call you when he wakes up? Then, if he's feeling all right, maybe you can get together and play later on."

Play, as if we were seven-year-olds.

I wandered back to my house, took the earring out of my pocket and stared at it.

Maybe Toby was right and it had nothing at all to do with the crime. I remembered the Sherlock Holmes stories I'd read and tried to think of how the great detective would approach the situation. Of course, he'd know the kind of metal the earring was made of and what shops sold it, and then he'd probably deduce something about the person who wore it from the style, itself.

But since it was the dead woman's, there seemed little to be gained from that angle: her several facets were already becoming known.

It even occurred to me that I didn't know whether it was real gold or gold plate. Probably the latter, of course, because nothing was real gold any more, but weren't there grades of purity? There was 14 karat, which was what everybody talked about, and then there was the cheap, painted stuff you got at Woolworth's. And I didn't have the expertise to tell the difference.

I put the object in the little tin box with a slot in the top where I saved my pennies and wished I'd roused myself to ask for the car. Without it, I was stuck.

I was still staring, red-eyed, at the little coin bank when I heard a car stop outside and a door slammed. I roused myself and went to the front door.

Blaize was coming up the sidewalk and I saw his mother waiting behind the wheel of the yellow Olds.

I opened the door and she waved.

I waved back.

"Mom said you came over a little while ago," he said.

His mother was already motioning for me to approach the car.

She leaned across the seat toward the still open door.

"Colin, when I told Blaize you'd come by he absolutely insisted that I bring him over. I certainly hope you aren't planning anything strenuous."

I noticed she was made up now, the pale cheeks heavily rouged and the smudges under her eyes gone. She'd even festooned herself with jewelry and I wondered where she was heading.

"I was just going to hang around here and watch TV," I said.

"That's fine. I'll rely on you. Blaize, you remember you have piano practice at three. Here, let me give you some money in case you decide to go down to the drugstore for a hotdog."

I watched him take the money and shove it quickly into his pocket. He hurried into the house and closed the door after us. The car pulled off and he gave a little shrug.

"How're you feeling?" I asked.

He looked up, surprised. "Fine. Oh, she told you . . ."

My turn to shrug. "She just said you had a little episode, she called it."

"God damn it," he said, his face red. "Why can't she leave me alone? I may have asthma, but I'm not dying."

"Sorry," I said.

"It isn't your fault."

We went back to my room.

"Look, there's something I want to show you," I said, "but you have to keep it to yourself."

He licked his lips and I saw his body stiffen.

"What do you mean?"

I told him about my excursion with Toby.

"I wouldn't believe him about anything," Blaize said with unusual vehemence. "I think all that about what his father says is stuff he invented anyway, just to make himself important."

"I don't know why I ended up with him last night. I guess I just wanted to show him . . ."

"You don't have to show him anything. You're worth ten of that fat son-of-a-bitch."

I hesitated, caught up short.

"Hell, Blaize . . ."

"I didn't mean to embarrass you, Colin. I know you aren't supposed to say things like that, because only queers say that kind of stuff. Is that what you were thinking?"

"No. I just . . . Forget it."

"Well, I'm not queer, if that's what you were wondering."

"I wasn't, so shut up and listen." I told him about the earring and then I opened the little box and handed it to him. He took it reverently, eyes large as dinner plates, and his hand started to shake.

"It's hers," he said.

"Hers?"

He hesitated and then gave a little shrug. "I saw her wearing them in class. I remember thinking how they didn't seem like her but . . ."

The phone interrupted and I heard my father's voice.

"Colin, listen to what I'm saying: I want you to stay where you are and don't go anywhere until I get there. I'll be home in five minutes."

"What's this about?" I'd never heard such urgency in his voice before.

"Some men may come there. From the police. I don't want you to say a word until I get home, is that understood?"

"Yes, sir."

The phone went dead and I stared blankly at Blaize.

"That was my dad. He says the cops are coming here."

My friend's mouth went open. "Shit."

I took the earring from him and replaced it in the tin box.

"Toby," I said. "That shit told his old man where we went last night. You'd better get out of here."

"No."

"Man, you don't want to get caught in this. If that earring was hers, it's evidence and I fucked with it."

"I don't care. I'm not leaving you."

I put a hand on his shoulder and only moved it when I heard car doors slamming a second later.

Two doors slamming. Two people.

Something melted in my guts. I looked over at the little box.

"I'll take care of it," Blaize said suddenly, reaching into the box and removing the earring. "In case they want to search."

"Shit, man, I don't want you to get your ass in a trap because of me."

"Shut up," he said quietly. He took a step toward me, his dark eyes fixing my own: "The earring was never here, okay? You never saw it. Whatever Toby told them was a lie."

"But if it's part of a crime . . ."

"It isn't, though. It belonged to her and it doesn't have anything to do with the crime."

"But fingerprints . . ."

"You handled it and now I've handled it. That will have wiped out anybody else's prints."

I heard the doorbell ring and then another car door closed. My father . . .

"I'm leaving the back way," Blaize said. "I'll be at my house. You can tell me what happened."

"I owe you," I said.

"We all owe each other," he said.

Before I could reply he was gone and the front door was opening. I stood helpless, like a deer pinioned in a spotlight. I saw my father, his face drawn. Behind him came two men, one skinny, with a loose tie and a coat that sloped off his narrow shoulders. The second man was more substantial, the size of a linebacker, and he was chewing gum. The first man flipped a cigarette butt into the bushes as he entered, as if he were about to get down to business.

"This is my son Colin," my father said. "If you'd like to sit down we can talk in here."

The big man eyed the skinny man but the latter nodded.

"That's fine."

My father turned to me.

"Colin, these men are from the sheriff's office. They want to talk to you about something that's supposed to have happened last night. You can sit down if you want but I expect you will tell them the absolute truth."

I swallowed.

"We hear you went out to the place where your teacher was killed last night," the skinny one said. His voice was high-pitched and he kept sniffing, as if he had an allergy.

"She wasn't my teacher . . ." I began but the big one cut me off:

"Son, you get wise, we'll find a place for you at LTI."

Louisiana Training Institute was the juvenile detention center and though I didn't know anyone who'd ever been there,
we'd all heard stories . . .

"I don't think we need to hear about LTI right now," my father
said. He looked me in the eye:

"Colin, did you go out to that place last night?"

"Yes, sir."

"With whom?"

I looked at the floor.

"Don't matter," the thin one said. "Your friend, the Hobbs
boy, got caught by his father climbing in his window. His father
got the truth out of him. Now we want to hear your side, before
we decide where to go with this."

"We were there," I mumbled.

"How did you get there?" the big one demanded.

"I drove," I said, my voice weak.

My father's head gave a little shake, as if to let me know how
disappointed he was.

"Whatever possessed you?" he asked.

I shrugged. "It was for Stan. We thought maybe we'd see
something that could help. We don't think his father did it."

The two detectives exchanged glances.

"And did you find anything?" the thin one asked.

I looked away. "Nothing important."

"You let us decide what's important," the big one snapped.

"Just some stuff. A woman's earring in the bushes."

"Where is it?"

I thought of Blaize and his good deed. I was damned if I'd be
like Toby and drag him in.

"I threw it out," I said.

"The Hobbs boy said you kept it." He leaned toward me like a
mountain about to fall.

"I threw it out on the way home, after I dropped him."

"You know what happens when you lie to the police," the thin one said.

"Yes, sir."

"We don't want you to get in any deeper than you already are," he said.

"... which is pretty deep, trespassing on a crime scene, removing evidence," his partner said.

"Like I said, I threw it away," I said. "If I'd have known it was important . . ."

"We're trying to help you," the thin one said. "But you have to understand, son, we're investigating a murder."

"You boys were out there the night it happened," the big man said. "Pretty interesting coincidence."

I shrugged again. "I told that deputy what we saw."

"Did you?" the big one said.

My father reached for his pipe and all at once I had a sense that I might not go to LTI after all.

"Was there anything marking this as a crime scene?" he asked. "I mean, that said for people to keep out?"

"Everybody knows it was a crime scene," the thin one said, taken aback. "And there's a NO TRESPASSING sign on the gate."

"But there's no closed gate, as I recall," my father said. "And if I remember correctly, that sign was put up by the property owner."

"That's right," the big man said. "Which means your son was trespassing."

My father nodded slowly, and lit his pipe. "Has the owner of the property complained?"

The two men exchanged looks again.

"Well, no," the thin one said. "But the crime scene . . ."

"How long does a place stay a crime scene?" my father asked. "I mean, don't the police put up some signs or something? Surely a place can't be a crime scene forever?"

"No, not forever," the thin one said. "But the investigation's not finished and . . ."

"But you gentlemen were finished with the investigation of that particular location, weren't you? Or you would have put up something to tell people to keep away."

"Dr. Douglas, you know as well as we do that your boy had no business out there last night. All we're asking is for you to cooperate, the way the Hobbs boy's father co-operated."

"Certainly. That's why I've invited you in to discuss this with my son. You're welcome to search, for that matter. I'm sure he doesn't have anything to hide. And, after all, you've made your arrest. Or was that a mistake?" Before either man could answer my father rose. "Gentlemen, I'm not happy with what Colin did and I promise you, I'll handle it. But you know how boys are. I'll bet you every teenager in the parish has been by that place since the murder. Some may even have walked around the cemetery. Summer school's starting in a few days and I can assure you Colin will be too busy to be making any more midnight excursions, besides the fact that he won't be doing much driving for the rest of the summer. Now, is it your intention to charge him and the Hobbs boy? I mean, after all, you'll have to charge both of them, because they were both involved. Because if that is your intention, I'd like to call my attorney now."

The two detectives seemed to draw into themselves, as if they'd been suddenly deflated. The thin one got up slowly. His partner seemed more reluctant, but at last he followed suit.

"All right," the thin one said. "There won't be any charges for right now. But we expect you to keep your boy under control."

My father showed them to the door and only closed it when their car pulled away from the curve. He turned slowly to face me.

"Colin, what in the hell's going on?"

"Nothing. I mean, we were just curious. We don't want Stan's dad to . . ."

"I feel as sorry as hell for Stanley. But Stan's dad has made his own bed and now he has to lie in it."

"You think he's guilty?"

My father exhaled. "Son, I don't know. I wish I did. At first none of us wanted to believe it. But things have been coming out, a little bit at a time, things that, well . . ."

"I know."

His brows arched. "Yes, I expect you do. Your grapevine may be better than our own. It seems like kids know things these days before grownups. But, damn it, Colin, I've told you about hanging around with Toby Hobbs. I'm sure he put you up to this."

I dropped my gaze.

"Or maybe you just wanted to enjoy your new driver's license, is that it? I can understand that, though I abhor deception."

"Yes, sir."

"But do you know what I abhor even more?"

I shook my head.

"Stupidity. The least you could have done was told him not to smoke in the car. It reeked of cigarettes. That doesn't say much for the intelligence of either of you."

They were the most scathing words I'd ever heard from my father and I felt as if I'd shrunk in size until I was a few inches off the floor.

"And another thing," he said, pointing his pipe at me like a gun: "Those policemen couldn't do anything because they'd have to have done something to Toby, and they know his father's in a position to make it hard for them, but they knew you were lying, and I do, too."

I didn't say anything, just let the fear seep through me.

"I . . ." But I stopped before I got started.

"Oh, I don't think it's about anything important. I know you didn't have anything to do with that crime and I don't think any of your friends did. But there's something else you're hiding. I won't pry into it because I doubt it's important. What's more important is that you've taken advantage of me and my trust."

"I'm sorry," I said. "It was the earring. Toby was right. I did find it."

"Where?"

I explained and my father listened intently, pulling on his pipe and sending clouds of aromatic smoke throughout the room.

"A gold earring with a star," he repeated. "For pierced ears?"

"I guess. I mean, I reckon I didn't really notice."

"Fine detective you are." He sat quietly for a long time, staring into the smoke. Finally he turned back to me:

"Where is it now?"

"I gave it to somebody."

"Blaize," he said, nodding, and sighed.

"How did you know?"

"Toby would have given it up and you haven't seen Stanley for several days. Who else does that leave?"

"Dad, please don't get him in trouble. He didn't have anything to do with this. He was just doing me a favor."

My father sighed and put a hand up to his face, as if he were in the throes of a major decision. At last he brought his hand down.

"'No mask like open truth to cover lies, As to go naked is the best disguise.'"

"What?"

"William Congreve, but you probably haven't ever heard of him."

"Yes, I have. He has a poem in our English book."

"Mirabile dictu. Well, I expect you'd better get Blaize to give you back that earring and then you hand it over to me. I'll keep it until I can see whether it's relevant or not. I don't intend for my son to get involved in something he had no part in just because of teenaged stupidity. But if it turns out the object would change the course of the investigation—save an innocent man, for example—then it will have to be produced."

"Yes, sir."

"Now you'd better call Blaize and get it back." He got up and accompanied me to the telephone.

But when I got Blaize he told me he'd thrown it down a sewer.

"I just figured we were all better off if it disappeared," he said. "Is there a problem?"

"No."

When I told my father he stroked his chin.

"Do you think he's telling the truth?"

"He wouldn't lie to me."

"No, I'm sure he wouldn't."

That night I got up to go to the bathroom and saw the light in the breakfast room was on. I smelled the aromatic smoke that told me my father was up. I caught just the outline of his back, seated in one of the straight wooden chairs, and then I tiptoed back to my room, lifted the window, and peed through the screen into the bushes outside.

When I woke up the next morning for the first day of summer school my father told me that Stan was missing.

CHAPTER FIFTEEN

I rise this morning determined that today I will meet the demons. I have been here for two days and I have as yet not summoned the courage to visit the place where it happened. I dress and go downstairs into the sunlight, determined to let nothing interfere, not even the rumblings in my stomach.

It's so easy, after all: just take the River Road from where it starts under the new bridge and follow.

And that is what I do, this warm summer morning, driving slowly along with the green levee on my right, past the frame houses, the campus incinerator, the new Veterinary Medicine Center. There is almost no traffic, though the road has long since been paved. I wonder, as I glance out at the purple flowers dotting the sides of the levee, and pass occasional bicyclists, if I will even recognize the place. The store has probably been torn down.

But the odometer has just marked four miles when I see it ahead on the left, the same gray-board, tin-roofed structure that I remember. Except that as I near it I see the gas pumps are gone and the front window is boarded. No one lives there now but ghosts. Bergeron must have died long ago and as for Michelle . . .

• • •

That morning I had to ask my father to repeat himself.

"I just heard it a little while ago," he said, knotting his tie. "I had to call Paul Terry about next fall's schedule and he told me he'd heard it from the campus police."

"But when?" I asked, thunderstruck.

"Last night, apparently. His mother went to wake him up and he was gone. His bed hadn't been slept in."

"I should have gone over," I said.

"Well, there are lots of things we should have done in retrospect, but I imagine he'll be all right. He probably just took off someplace to think things over."

"But where? He doesn't have any money."

"He can't go far. His mom will be out looking for him, as well as the police."

"But what if somebody kidnapped him?"

"I think you're letting your imagination run wild. Now you'd better get dressed and get some breakfast. I plan to leave as soon as I finish reading the paper."

I stared down into my raisin bran. Stan gone. Why the hell hadn't I gone over there and at least offered comfort?

"I'm sorry your dad killed Miss Gloria. I'm still your friend."

Sure. That would have worked fine. Still, I couldn't get that night out of my mind: His mother following his father out, yelling after him, and Stan morose in his little room that wasn't even a part of the house, as if he'd been exiled so that he would not have to witness what went on in the domestic circle. I'd always thought it was great, having his own place, but now I saw it from a different perspective.

The summer course I'd enrolled in was a typing class that lasted from nine until eleven. It provided no school credit but my father said everyone should know how to type, and that it would stand me in good stead later, because no teacher wanted to read handwritten papers, and a paper that came in typed always made a better impression. But I knew the real reason for my enrollment was that it gave me something to do in the mornings.

I don't remember much about that first class meeting except that I heard nothing the earnest young graduate student instructor said, because my mind was on Stan.

Where would I go if I were he?

There was just one answer: I would go where we always went to get away, to where you could lie by the river and smell the mud and hear the wash of the waves and turn your face up to the sky and pretend you were one of the hawks circling overhead on the currents of air. I knew that if I just went to the levee I would find him. Then I'd sit beside him and let him talk it all out, not saying anything, just listening, the way a friend should, and when he was finished and it had all spilled free, then we'd get up and I'd take him home, or maybe I'd take him to my place, if he felt more comfortable there, because I knew my father wouldn't object.

That's why, when the class was over, I walked from the basement of Himes Hall, where we met, and past the new library to Allen Hall, which housed the English Department. I climbed the steps to the second floor, and found my father in his office. His door was half-closed and through it I heard him talking to someone in a low voice.

". . . really like to see you," he was saying and I realized he was on the phone. I strained to hear who he was talking to, but all I heard was the word, "Good," and the phone being replaced in its cradle. I waited a few seconds, took a deep breath, and knocked on the frosted glass of the door.

"Yes?" he called in a slightly bored voice and then started when he saw me.

"Colin. Finished already?"

"Yes, sir."

"Well, if you can hang around the library for an hour I'll take you to get a hamburger at Louie's and then run you home."

I nodded. I was already formulating a plan.

"So did you learn some things?" he asked just over an hour later as we sat on stools in Louie's cramped little box of a café on Chimes Street, just across from the campus.

"Some," I said.

"I know it's boring at first, but, believe me, you'll be glad later."

"Yes, sir." I watched him out of the corner of my eye. Long ago he'd told me how he and my mother used to eat here, because the hamburgers and fries were the best in the world, and whenever we came here together, which was infrequently, I always had the sense that his mind was on those days.

"Dad," I said finally, as he picked up one of the last fries. His head came around slowly to look at me.

"Yes?"

"I'm sorry about the other night."

He nodded slowly. "I'm glad to hear it. It was a dumb thing to do, but everybody does dumb things sometimes. The trick is not to make it a habit."

"Yes, sir."

He popped the fry into his mouth and I waited while he chewed it.

"I've been thinking about Stan," I said, "trying to figure all the places he might be."

"Yes."

"I have some ideas."

"You want to tell me what they are?"

"I'd like to go look on the levee. I mean, that's where we always went. That's where I'd go."

He took a deep breath.

"Is that what this apology is about, then? You were working

up to try to get back your driving privileges?" He shook his head sadly. "I'd hate to think that."

"Dad, I know I did something stupid. But wouldn't you want somebody to come after me if I was missing?"

He nodded. "I guess I would. But I can drive you out there if that's what you want to do."

"Dad, if he's really run away, if he sees you or somebody else . . ." I played with what was left of my meal. "Besides, by then it'll be late, after four."

"I don't know what that's got to do with it. It stays light until nearly eight."

"But what if he decides to go somewhere else in the meantime?"

"Son, you're bound and determined to pry that car loose, aren't you?"

"I was just thinking about Stan."

He fished out his wallet and pulled out a dollar and some change.

"Thanks, Louie." He slid off the stool, exchanged pleasantries with a couple of university acquaintances a few stools down. We walked out into the heat and he hitched his trousers.

"Can you think of one single reason I ought to trust you?" he asked.

"No, sir. Except it isn't for me."

We walked across the street and back onto the campus.

"You've got a hell of a nerve," he said. "But I can't say I like the idea of Stanley being out there, either." He jerked his head in my direction: "You haven't talked to Toby Hobbs about this, have you?"

"No, sir."

"You just want to drive down to where you camp and look for him."

"Yes, sir."

We walked a few more steps while he mulled it.

"The water's high now," he said suddenly, with ill-concealed satisfaction. "He couldn't get across the borrow pit without his canoe."

"There are logs, fallen trees."

"Are there?"

"Yes, sir."

There was a thin sheen of sweat on his brow now, but I figured it was because we were walking in the midday sun.

He stopped suddenly.

"I may be crazy as hell, but here." He dug the car keys out of his pocket and dangled them in front of me.

"I want it absolutely understood you won't go anywhere near that cemetery."

"No, sir."

"Or near that man Sikes. And that when you go there, you'll walk over there, check your camping site, and not loiter around, just come right back."

"Yes, sir."

• • •

I stopped at Bergeron's to ask if he'd seen Stan, because if Stan was hungry the store was the nearest place for him to get food, but the storekeeper wasn't in evidence. Instead, to my surprise, the counter was being tended by Michelle.

"Where're your friends today?" she asked.

I shrugged. She'd never spoken to me directly, because I'd always hung back and let Stan or Toby do the talking. Now, with her sultry eyes on me, I felt my belly quivering.

"So when did you start driving?" she asked.

"Couple of days ago," I mumbled.

"And you're just out driving around?"

"Yeah."

"My dad won't let me get my license," she said. "Ain't that crappy?"

"I guess so." I got a Dr. Pepper out of the cooler and hunted in my pants for a nickel but she shook her head.

"It's okay. He ain't here."

"Thanks." I tried to imagine her with Toby but the image wouldn't jell.

"So why'd you really come here?" she asked, leaning over the counter. It was warm in the building and a faint muskiness seemed to mingle with the odors of dust and stale bread.

"I was looking for one of my friends."

"And you expect to find him here?"

"No," I said, indicating the levee with my head. "Over there. I thought maybe you'd seen him."

She considered and then smiled.

"May have," she said.

"When?" I asked.

"Not now. Come back later. Two-thirty. I'll show you then."

"You know where he is?"

"My dad'll be back in a minute, so you better go before he finds out I gave you a drink. Meet me on the other side of the levee, down where you camp, at two-thirty."

"You'll take me to him?"

"Sure."

• • •

Maybe, I thought, I should pick up Blaize, but when I went to his apartment his mother told me he had piano lessons and she knew he'd be sorry he'd missed me. I couldn't tell whether or not she'd heard that Stan was missing. I spent the rest of the time driving aimlessly around. The idea of meeting Michelle Bergeron on the other side of the levee sent tingles down my spine and I thought about what Toby had said, about how he'd been with her when the murder had happened. I hadn't believed him at the time and I didn't believe him now but something about the way she smiled at me made me wonder.

At two fifteen I rolled by Bergeron's store, noting that his pickup was outside now. I passed Windsong and the cemetery and drove up onto the levee at our usual place.

Maybe, I thought, Michelle had been bringing Stan food. That was all that made sense.

I stopped at the top, shut off the engine, and got out. I walked down to the edge of the borrow pit. The pit was a tangle of vines and tree limbs with just the single path we used for dragging the canoe to the water's edge. I looked around on the grass, to see if there was any sign of recent activity, but other than some cow manure and a used oil filter there was nothing.

I ventured down the path, brushing the limbs out of my face. Maybe she'd gone ahead of me. Then I heard movement behind me and froze.

When I turned around she was standing there, back to the levee, smiling. She wore cut-off jeans and a t-shirt against which her breasts pushed like twin basketballs and I gulped.

"You're early," she said.

"I guess so."

Before I could say anything else she slipped past me, heading toward the murky pit.

"Come on."

"Where are we going?"

"Across."

So she knew about the fallen tree.

I watched her pick her way along the log, arms held out on either side for balance.

"You're going to fall in," I said.

She laughed and grabbed a limb on the other side, pulling herself to the opposite bank.

She turned to face me from the other side of the water.

"Come on," she said.

"Is this where he is?" I asked.

"Who?"

"My friend. You said you were taking me to him."

"Oh, yeah. Come on."

I made my way along the log, took a deep breath, and hurried along the last three steps that left me without support. But then my hand, too, touched the limb on the other side and I guided myself onto the firm ground.

"Up here," she said, vanishing like a sylph into the weeds. I went after her, catching up in the clearing.

"I don't see him," I said.

Her face screwed up in displeasure. "What's so important about him? He's just a red-headed frog."

"You thought I was talking about Toby?"

"Toby, schmobie. I don't know his name."

"You don't know his name?"

"Why should I? I've never talked to you guys except when you come to the store."

"And you didn't go out with him the night of..?"

"Go out with him?" She laughed. "Are you serious?"

"No," I said and poked my shoe at the remains of our old campfire. I stooped and touched one of the burned logs. It was warm to the touch, but, then, it was a hot day and maybe the extra heat was just my imagination.

"I wonder if somebody else was here after us?" I asked.

She shrugged. "Tramps, maybe. All kinds of people come down here. That's why I had to sneak out. My old man is scared to death about me coming here since that happened."

I nodded. "I don't guess you saw or heard anything that night," I said.

"No. I was asleep. You were the ones who were out here, you and fatso and the other boy, the short one."

"Stan."

"Is that his name?"

"Yeah."

She shrugged.

"You haven't seen him?"

"Not since that night when he was with you. Look, why all the questions?"

"He disappeared."

Her eyes widened. "No shit. You think something happened to him?"

"I thought maybe he came down here."

"I haven't seen him. Look, he'll be okay."

"I guess."

"He *will*. I promise. Now tell me something . . ."

"What?"

She stepped toward me, brown eyes on my own. "No lies, okay?"

"Okay."

She reached out then and put both hands on my shoulders.

"You ever kissed a girl? I mean *really* kissed a girl?"

My stomach started to vibrate. "Sort of."

"What does that mean?" She was smiling now, and I couldn't will myself to move away.

"I . . ."

"Come here."

I stepped forward and she took my right hand in her own and guided it under her t-shirt until I was touching her breast. She turned my palm upward until I was cupping it and, rising on her tiptoes, pressed her mouth against mine. Her tongue sought my own, exploring my mouth, and I tentatively responded with my own tongue. She thrust her breast against my hand and I felt her nipple pressing my palm like a little helmet.

She reached for my other hand then, and, unsnapping her cut-offs, pushed my hand down between her legs until I found the soft nest of hair at the base of her belly.

She spread her legs slightly, insinuating my finger into her cleft and moaned.

A second later I felt her hand on the front of my jeans, kneading what had become a hard bulge in spite of myself.

She drew back slightly.

"This is your first time, isn't it?"

"Well . . ."

"That's okay. I'll show you. I'll put my shirt on the ground. I don't want to get grass all over my butt."

She pulled the t-shirt over her head, until her breasts bobbed free. I stared at them, paralyzed: They were huge, disproportionately so, and I wondered for a moment if she was malformed.

Then I caught something in the corner of my eye, a movement of white through the trees. I turned toward the levee, half-hidden by the jungle of trees.

"What is it?" she asked from behind me.

"I saw something."

"It's just your imagination. Come on."

But I had seen it, something that didn't belong. I walked down the slope to the edge of the borrow pit and parted the foliage.

• • •

I stared out over the brown, fetid water, at the green levee. I could just make out my car at the top and there, to my surprise, was a man on horseback, staring at the vehicle, like a matador confronting a bull. He had a beard and was maybe thirty, but that was all I could see.

"Jesus," I muttered.

"What is it?" Michelle called.

"A man . . ." I said.

"What?"

Even as I watched he dismounted, went over to the car, peered in the window.

"What's he doing?" she asked.

"Looking at my car." Almost as if he'd heard me, the man turned his head in my direction. I froze.

"I think he sees me." Even as I spoke he started down the levee, reins in hand, toward the edge of the borrow pit.

I heard her footsteps behind me and felt her nipples against my back.

"Let me see. Shit!" Her breath drew in.

"What is it?"

"Let's get out of here," she said, heading up the incline toward the camp spot.

"Maybe he'll go away," I said.

I let the foliage drop back into place. She was already pulling the t-shirt back over her head.

"Let's go," she whispered, motioning for me to follow. "We'll have to go out the hard way."

Before I could answer she was already plunging into the thicket, headed north along the batture on a little footpath that was little more than a game trail. I followed, wilted in more ways than one.

"Uhh, there's a spot here," I said, pointing to a little clearing.

"Forget it. There's probably spiders and red-bugs. Besides, he may find a way to get across."

Half an hour later we picked our way through the last batch of briars, emerging at the rim of the borrow pit. She found a mud bridge and I dutifully followed her across, watching her slip twice and streak her legs with mud. When we came out on the toe of the levee, she turned to me on one leg, reaching down to pick a sticker out of her ankle.

"The store's right on the other side. I've got to sneak back before my old man sees all this mud and asks where I've been. Last time he took after me with his strap."

"But Michelle . . ."

"Hey, sometimes it works, sometimes it doesn't." She put a hand on my shoulder. "Now do me a favor and don't walk up on top. I don't want him to see us up there together."

"Sure. But I can come back."

"Yeah, right, do that."

I watched the dream shatter as she started up the slope and away from me forever.

"Michelle . . ."

"What?" She didn't even stop.

"The man on the horse. Who was he?"

"Drood, you dummy. Darwin Drood."

CHAPTER SIXTEEN

I stare at the falling shack that was once Bergeron's. Through the streaked glass of the car window it has the quality of a movie, and I wonder if I am really here or whether reality is what I have been remembering, when I watched Michelle Bergeron disappear over the levee after letting me get so close. Then I wonder if perhaps what I remember hasn't been manufactured out of my writer's imagination. Maybe I didn't meet her that day. Maybe it was just something I wished had happened, because it has the surreal quality of which adolescent fantasies are made. And if I can deny it, then I can also deny what happened that day two months ago, when I sat behind another glass and watched a man die.

• • •

When I met my father at his office he asked if I'd found Stan and I told him no. He seemed thoughtful.

"No trace?" he asked.

"Nothing." I didn't tell him that I'd hardly spent my time examining the ground for traces, because a girl three years older than I had tried to get me to have sex with her.

"Odd. I thought you might have had something there. It does seem like a logical place to go."

I didn't say anything. On the way home he picked up the subject again:

"See anybody at all out there?"

"A man on a horse," I said. "They told me at Bergeron's it was Mr. Drood, from Windsong."

"Drood's showing himself, is he?" There was a note I didn't recognize in my father's voice. "Was he on Windsong?"

"No, down by the camping place." I described what I'd seen, leaving out the fact that I hadn't been alone.

My father shook his head. "Well, best you stay away from him."

"Why?"

"Just do what I say."

"Is it what you said happened when he was young? What was it?"

"I'm not sure and maybe it doesn't matter now. But you give the man a wide berth, understand?"

"Yes, sir."

· · ·

Ten minutes after we got home he came to my door.

"I have to go out for a little while. I should be back in plenty of time for supper."

With a surge of excitement I realized I was about to be alone. As soon as the car started I returned to my room and lay on the bed.

I'd gone to the levee to look for Stan but instead I'd found Michelle and we'd almost . . .

An image of her naked body hovered before me in the twilight of the room and in my imagination she was asking me to undress while she moved toward me.

My God, she'd let me touch her *there*.

My hand moved down again only instead of touching her body I felt myself touching my own.

I'd had erections before and seen guys in the locker room with them, as they traded dirty stories, but I knew the Church, in which I no longer professed any belief, condemned touching oneself in this way.

But surely there was no harm in a touch, in a few gentle squeezes, so long as I stopped short. After all, I'd had wet dreams, felt the intense sensation of pleasure that came from orgasm while I slept, and I knew I could control myself.

Except that I couldn't and before I could stop myself I felt the sudden rush of sensation as my seed shot out onto my belly and chest. I closed my eyes, letting the sensations die away.

I'd done it now. Mortal sin. There was no going back.

• • •

I was cleaned up by the time my father returned, his face screwed up in worry. I'd seldom seen him like this, but I didn't know how to ask him what was the matter.

I tried to force myself to think of Stan and where he might be, but my mind kept returning to Michelle. There had to be a way to get back there, maybe take her out in the car, do it in the back seat like I'd heard other guys saying they did it with their dates.

Damn, what kind of person was I? I hadn't gone to see Stan when he needed me and now, instead of worrying about him, I was fantasizing about a girl who'd let me feel her up.

It was after supper and I was watching TV when the phone rang. I got to it before my father and heard Toby's voice.

"So what's happening, cat?"

I looked around to make sure my father wasn't within hearing distance.

"Screw you," I said. "You told the cops about the earring. They came here and questioned me, you bastard."

"Hey, don't get pissed. My old man caught me coming in. What was I supposed to do?"

"You didn't have to say anything about the fucking earring."

"Shit on you, jack. I'm not concealing evidence."

"You're a damn hypocrite and you're a liar, besides. I talked to Michelle and she said you weren't with her that night. So maybe you've got something to hide, and maybe I ought to rat on you."

"You're a lying fuck. You didn't talk to Michelle. She wouldn't say 'Kiss my ass' to you."

"You don't think?"

"Man, you're full of it."

"Ask her then."

"I don't have to."

"Okay. Just proves my point. You're the one she wouldn't talk to."

He was silent and I heard a Dell Shannon record in the background.

"You didn't really talk to her," he said.

"Okay, I didn't really talk to her."

"When the fuck would you have had time?"

"When I drove out today to look for Stan. Michelle was by herself in the store."

"Shit, that ain't no big deal. What were you doing looking for Stan there?"

"I thought he might have gone to hide out on the levee."

"And did he?"

"I didn't see him."

Then, for some reason, I thought about the recent campfire. Michelle had attributed it to tramps, but it could just as well have been Stan. If I hadn't been thinking about getting laid . . .

"I saw Darwin Drood, though," I told him.

"What was he doing?"

"Riding his horse. Except that he got off and came down to the borrow pit, like he was looking for something—or somebody."

"So maybe he was looking for a place to fuck his horse."

"You're a pain in the ass. All this shit about how you find out shit from your old man and you don't know crap."

"I wouldn't start talking about anybody's old man, dick-wit. Not after what I saw just now."

"What are you trying to say?"

"Nothing. I'd just like to know what your old man was doing with Stan's mom before supper today."

"What?"

"You heard me. I drove by to see if maybe Stan came back. I was gonna walk back to his hut if no cars were there. But there wasn't just one car there, there was two. Stan's mom's and your old man's. So I thought maybe he really *did* come back and you were over there, which is why I called. But since you *weren't* there, that just leaves one other possibility. Your old man is dicking Stan's old lady while Stan's old man's in jail."

CHAPTER SEVENTEEN

When I got rid of Toby I sat staring at the phone.

It wasn't true. It was just another of Toby's lies. My father couldn't . . . I snatched up the phone again and called Blaize.

"I need to talk to you," I said.

His voice was low, as if his mother was nearby.

"Can you come by later?

"How much later?"

"After eleven. She'll be asleep then. Knock on my window."

"All right." I hung up, glimpsing my father in his shirt-sleeves, reading a book while the radio played classical music. He hadn't even removed his tie, as if he were still on duty. I tried to imagine him sweating in the arms of Mrs. Chandler, but the image wouldn't jell.

I wandered into the living room.

"You didn't hear anything about Stan, did you?" I asked.

He looked up from the book and nudged his glasses up on his nose.

"Why, no. I have to say I'm a little worried."

I waited for him to tell me that was why he'd gone to see Mrs. Chandler, but he offered nothing. I nodded and went back to my own room, locking the door behind me.

He was the neatest man I'd ever seen and there was still hardly a crease in his shirt. If he'd been making love to Stan's mom, wouldn't it be wrinkled? But then I realized he would have taken it off, hung it on a hanger. That was his way.

At ten-thirty I heard his bedroom door close and I turned out my own light. Half an hour later I slipped into the hallway. The window unit blocked out any sound from inside his room but there was no light from under the door. I waited another fifteen minutes, then went out my window and walked down the dark street to Blaize's apartment.

They lived on the ground floor and his room was in the rear corner. I made my way silently across the grass, alert to any signs of life. A couple of the upstairs units had lit windows but the place next door was dark. I stood on tiptoes under his window and rapped lightly with my knuckles.

Almost immediately the pane was raised and Blaize stuck his head out.

"Can you get in?" he asked.

"It's kind of high."

"Here." He reached out, leaning over the sill, and I grabbed his wrists. He pulled, grunting with the effort, and I reached out with one hand and grabbed the sill.

For a few seconds I floundered, half in and half out but his hand came down, seized my belt, and helped pull me the rest of the way in. I tumbled onto the floor atop him, and for a second we lay there, huffing in the Lysol-scented blackness like exhausted lovers. I slowly disengaged and rubbed my forearms, where the sill had scraped them raw.

"You okay?" he asked.

"Yeah. You want to shut the window?"

"Actually, no. I like the night air. When my mom goes to sleep I open the window all the time, just to breathe in the fresh air. Once I forgot and it was open in the morning and she gave me hell."

"You sure she's asleep now?"

"Nothing would wake her up. She always takes a bunch of pills. She says she can't sleep without them."

I could barely make him out in the darkness, but then the headlights of a passing car raked the trees outside, reflected dimly off his face, and I was aware of his eyes on me.

"You probably wonder why I'm here," I asked.

"Yeah. But I figure you've got a reason."

"There was: there's nobody else I can talk to."

"I know how that feels."

"Right." I hesitated, trying to decide how to say it.

"Look, Blaize, let me ask you: if you knew somebody real well, I mean like forever, and you figured you knew that person in and out, do you think they could do anything that would surprise you?"

"You mean could you do anything that would surprise me, and vice versa?"

"No, I mean if you knew somebody better than that."

"I think anybody could surprise anybody else."

"Serious?"

"Sure. I mean, how much do we really know about anybody else, really? How much do we know about ourselves? You may say, 'I wouldn't do this or that,' but how do you know until you're facing it head on? I think anybody's capable of anything."

"Jesus."

"You asked."

Then I told him about my father and what Toby had said.

"I just can't see it being true," I said. "Sure, he's been alone for a long time and I guess he needs it sometimes, but Stan's mom . . ?"

When he answered, his voice was cold and analytical:

"Colin, if you're asking whether I think it's possible your dad's screwing Stan's mom, the answer's yes. And for the reasons you mentioned. But that doesn't mean I think it's true. Those are two different things."

I felt the weight lift slightly.

He went on: "You're quoting Toby. That sorry sack of shit would say anything. He was pissed because you jumped him for telling his dad about the earring. So he had to get back. There's all sorts of reasons your dad could have been at Stan's house."

"I know. It's just . . ."

"Just what? Because Toby said it or because you really deep down think it may be true?"

"I heard him talking to somebody on the telephone in a low voice this morning. I heard him say he had to see them, whoever he was talking to."

"So? Maybe it was Stan's mom, maybe it wasn't. But so what if it was? He's worried about Stan, too. Maybe he went over there to see how she was doing. To ask if she's heard anything. Look, Toby just saw the car, he didn't see anybody with their pants down."

"No."

"So I wouldn't worry about it."

I nodded in the darkness. It was what I'd wanted to hear.

"It's Stan we ought to be worried about," Blaize said.

Then I told him how I'd tried to find Stan and how I'd been diverted by Michelle Bergeron.

"I swear to God," I finished.

"I believe you," he said simply.

"You do? I mean, that Michelle actually let me..?"

"I said so. The problem isn't what you did with her anyway. The problem's that you didn't follow up. You said somebody had been to the camp site."

I lowered my eyes, even though I doubted he could see them in the darkness. "I know."

"Look, Colin, shit happens, okay? You just can't let it paralyze you."

"You're right. But I don't know where to go from here."

"I do."

I slowly looked up, shaken by the certainty in his voice.

"It's simple," he said. "You go wherever's left to go."

"And where's that?"

"Back to Michelle."

"Are you serious?"

"She likes you, right? She lives there, right? You think Stan could hide on the levee without her knowing?"

I shrugged.

"We need to ask her again. Make her tell what she knows."

"We?"

"Stan's my friend, too. He can't help whatever his father did or didn't do. But we have to find him before something bad happens."

"Like what?"

"I don't know. But there was something about Drood that scared her, right? She didn't say she was scared of Sikes, just Drood. So what is it about the two of them? What's the connection? Is Sikes protecting Drood or is Drood taking care of Sikes? I bet there's something she knows about them, something she may have gotten from her father. And if Stan's out there some place, we ought to know, too."

I exhaled. "You're right. I should have made her tell me when we were together."

"Should have, could have. Don't worry about that. It's what we've got to do now." He paused for a second, thinking.

"Reckon your father will let you have the car again tomorrow after your class?"

"If I say I'm looking for Stan."

"Then pick me up and we'll drive to the store and see if Michelle's by herself."

"You can get loose?"

"My mom has a book club meeting. I'll leave a note and tell her I'm with you." His tone took a wry note: "She approves of you."

• • •

It didn't take much to get the car the next afternoon. My punishment had seemingly withered away and when I told my father I had some more ideas about where to look for Stan, he nodded and wished me good luck.

Blaize was right: What Toby had told me was crap and I should have known it to begin with.

I picked Blaize up and we drove back out through the university to the River Road.

"What if she isn't alone?" I asked. "What if she isn't even there?"

"Then we buy a Coke and leave and come back later."

"And then?"

"Let's get there first."

I needn't have worried. She was there, and as alone as the day before. I left Blaize in the car and went in. She looked up from her comic book.

"Hey," she said with a knowing smile.

"Hey," I said, embarrassed by the bulge in my pants.

"I can't leave right now," she said without my asking. "And my mama asked me all kinds of questions about how I got so muddy. They've been watching me ever since."

"That's okay," I said. "I . . ."

"No, it's not. It's shitty," she said. "I'll be so glad to get away from this place."

"Look . . ."

"Come back tonight," she said quickly, cutting me off. "Come back at eleven-thirty. I'll be waiting in the backyard. When I see you I'll run out and get into the car."

I nodded. "Right."

I was turning away to go, legs jelly, when the front door opened and Blaize walked in.

"I thought you were alone," Michelle accused.

"This is Blaize. He was waiting in the car."

"Blaize? You mean like in St. Blaize, the guy who cures throat problems? The one where the priest comes around with the two candles and puts them against your neck?"

"Yeah, that one," Blaize said.

Michelle glared at me. "*Why did you bring him? What did you tell him? If you think . . .*"

"He didn't tell me anything," Blaize said. "Except that he thinks our friend Stan may be down here camping on the levee."

"What's that got to do with me?"

"You see everything that goes on here. Colin thought you might have seen him and I think so, too."

"I don't care what you think, skinny boy."

"You can call me whatever you want. But at least I've got two friends, and if one of them is in danger, I want to help him, and if you had any friends, you'd feel the same way."

"I have plenty of friends."

"Then would you want them hurt?"

Michelle screwed up her face and I didn't know if she was going to yell at us or cry.

"Colin said there was a fresh campfire on the levee. Was it Stan?"

Michelle threw back her hair. "I don't know what his name is. I don't know any of your names."

"But you saw him," Blaize persisted.

"I saw him. But it was a couple of days ago. I haven't seen him since."

"Is he in danger?" I asked.

"How should I know?"

"Because something about Drood scared you."

"You did tell him," she accused.

"I told him Drood came along and you spooked."

"That's cause he's spooky," she shot back.

"It isn't because of something that happened a long time ago?" Blaize asked.

"You've got to get out of here. If my old man comes, he'll think I've been . . ."

"Just tell us about Drood," Blaize said. "We'll leave."

"I don't know about Drood," she cried, lip trembling. "I only know what my parents say."

"And what's that?" Blaize asked.

"That they're a screwed-up bunch of people, okay? That they're all crazy."

"Something happened when Darwin Drood was younger," I said. "He got sent up north afterwards. What was it?"

"I don't goddamn know! I don't mess with the Droods or Sikeses or any of those folks. My daddy told me to keep away and I do. He said they was all screwed up and it didn't do nobody no good to get mixed up with them."

"He must have said other things," I said.

"I told you he didn't say shit. Now get out of here before we all get in trouble. Please."

"There's nothing else you know about Drood?" I asked, desperate.

"Nothing." She gave a little shrug. "Unless you count what Sikes said when he was drinking."

"What?" Blaize and I said it together.

"It was a long time ago, back when my folks were still talking to Sikes. He used to get drunk and come around and my daddy had to keep throwing him out and finally it got so bad they had a showdown and Sikes didn't come no more."

"But what did he say?" I asked.

"It didn't make no sense. My daddy told me just to shut up my ears. I mean, I was just a little girl then."

"What did Sikes say?"

"I don't know. Something crazy. My daddy told him to stay away from us kids and Sikes said it was Drood he ought to be worried about, something about 'After what Drood done to my son somebody ought to kill him.'"

"Oh, Jesus," I said.

"Why?" she demanded. "What difference does that make?"

"Because of Stan," I said, reaching out to grab her by the shoulders. "Don't you see? If he does things to kids, he might do something to Stan."

"I didn't think of that."

"I didn't think about Drood," I admitted, turning to Blaize. "All this time I was thinking about Sikes. But it might have been Drood who killed Miss Gloria. And if he killed her, and he's done things to other kids, then who knows what he'd do to Stan?"

Michelle tried to twist free, then gave up.

I faced her again: "If Drood has him, where would he take him?"

"I don't know. Probably the old house."

"Windsong?"

"Maybe. Or maybe the sugar house."

"The sugar house?"

"Yeah, it's all tumbled down, but there's part of it still standing. We used to play like it was a fort when I was little. Me and the little nigger kids used to sneak in until Sikes would run us off. They started saying it was because he buried bodies back there, but I never saw none."

"We have to check it out," Blaize said. "We can't just go off and leave him."

"You're going there?" Michelle asked, her face white. "You're crazy."

"Come on," Blaize said.

I let Michelle go and we started out of the store.

We'd reached the gas pumps when the front door creaked open.

"Wait . . ." she called. "You really going back there looking?"

"When it's dark," I said.

She bit her lip, as if trying to decide something.

"You don't know the path," she said.

"You can see it from the road," I said. "We'll go over the fence."

"No. There's a path from the old graveyard. It takes you behind the first fence lines. It's easier."

"We'll look for it," I said.

"Wait," she cried again, as I opened the car door.

"What?"

"Be at the graveyard at midnight," she said. "I'll take you."

CHAPTER EIGHTEEN

Michelle, where are you now? A grandmother eight times over? The gray matriarch, long gone to fat, whose memories dim with each passing day? Or do you perhaps sometimes think back to that day on the levee? Do you confuse me in your memory with the faces of all the others? Even after what happened? And would you recognize me now? Would you want to talk to me, or would you avoid me, afraid I'd ask you to explain?

I know one thing: That is that even this many years later the image of her will never fade. She will always be what she was then, knowing, sultry, and more than a little afraid.

• • •

When I got back with the car it was making a strange sound. My father listened and I went with him to the filling station on Dufroq Street, where the mechanic opened the hood and pronounced the timing chain ready to give up the ghost. He told us it was a good thing we hadn't been on the highway, because not only would the engine have suddenly quit, but the motor itself would have locked up.

We left the car in his care, because he said we'd be taking a chance to drive it another block, and we walked home, through the Garden District. My father said tomorrow we'd get a ride from one of his colleagues. To my relief, he didn't ask me what I'd done to the car.

I called Blaize when we got home.

"There's no way to get to the levee now," I told him. "Unless we call Toby."

"I don't want to fool with him," Blaize said.

"I don't either. But what else can we do?"

There was a long silence and then he said:

"I know where my mother keeps the keys."

"You mean use your car?"

"What choice do we have?"

"But you don't even know how to drive."

"You can drive it. Just don't go fast."

"But if she wakes up and the car's gone . . ."

"I told you, she takes things to make her sleep."

I exhaled. After a few more seconds of silence I nodded into the phone.

"Okay."

• • •

And that's how, at eleven-thirty, I came to be driving the long yellow Olds, choking from the smell of perfume that seemed to saturate the interior. It was as if Blanche St. Martin was in the car with us, hovering from the back seat, and I know Blaize felt it, too.

"It'll be okay," he said. "If we find him, nobody'll blame us for anything, because we did what none of them could do."

"Yeah," I said, but there was still a gnawing in the pit of my belly.

• • •

Standing here now in the hammering sun I wonder how we ever nerved ourselves to do it. And what if we hadn't? How would things have come out then? That is the one question that obsesses me the most, the question I have come here in hopes of answering. Because if we hadn't gone out that night, if I had accepted the hint from fate, which caused my father's car to be broken, then I would have recognized that this was not meant to be. Call it God, destiny, or whatever: I, the lifelong agnostic, have labored all these years with the biting doubt that I ignored a sign from on high.

I have tried to reconcile it with the realization that, by myself, I never would have mustered the courage, that the courage came from Blaize, who perhaps had his own manhood to prove. That left alone I would have stayed in that night and things would have turned out differently. I would have spent the rest of my life harboring a small doubt as to my own loyalty to friends, but that would have been a small price to pay.

Price for what? Things turned out all right, didn't they? I am alive and Blaize is alive and justice was done. Is that an outcome to ignore? Or is it that I have harbored doubts all these decades? That perhaps my own memory has been pressed into the service of these doubts, so that at this point I cannot even be certain of what happened, and Blaize, with his own demons to combat, is not willing to awaken them in order to tell me?

• • •

The store was a black lump as we passed it, the tires making popping sounds on the gravel. I wondered if Michelle was watching from somewhere inside the darkened structure. I wondered if she would even come at all.

There was no sign of life from Windsong, either, and the Sikes place was closed up tight, the red truck sitting in the front yard beside the broken-down Belair.

I reached the cemetery road and turned in, careful to keep the big car from sliding in the loose dirt.

"She won't come," I said, cutting the headlights so that all we had to guide us were the dimmers.

We reached the end of the road and I looked over at Blaize. We were thinking the same thing: Our last chance to leave. It only needed one of us to shake his head, tell the other this was a bad idea. But he only gave a little nod.

I cut the engine and hit the dimmer switch.

The night fell over us like a tent, suffocating with the heat of a day that had died hard. A smell of hay, mixed with the dank odor of earth, emanated from the graveyard. Crickets chirped and then the chirping stopped.

I stood on the little track, half in and half out of the car, then eased the door closed to shut off the interior light.

And saw her.

She was rising up from the tombstones, just like before, a wraith, beckoning, coming toward me. I tried to run, but my legs refused to work. Then I heard Blaize's voice.

"It's Michelle."

She came toward us then and halted.

"I didn't think you'd come," I said.

She stared from Blaize to me, and then her fist flew to her mouth, as though stifling a scream. She lurched past us and I saw her form vanish into the darkness of the road.

"What the hell?" I asked.

"I don't know," Blaize said. "Something scared her."

"You reckon it was something in the graveyard?" I asked.

A shrug.

I took out my flashlight, hand shaking.

What if there'd been another murder?

"Maybe we should . . ." But the words choked in my throat. It was too late now. We started forward together, scanning the ground with the flash. But there was nothing—no body, no blood, no sign of anything out of the normal.

"You think it could be a trap?" I asked.

"Why? What could Michelle have to do with it?"

"I don't know. But it's kind of like up on the levee yesterday. She took one look at Drood and spooked."

"Do you see Drood here?" Blaize asked.

"You're right."

I used my light to guide us to the little gate at the far side of the cemetery. Sure enough, a path led out through the pasture, vanishing into the darkness.

"This must be the path to the sugar house ruin," I said. "If she was telling the truth."

He nodded. "Better shut off the light, though."

I flipped off the flashlight and we started out in single file. Overhead the moon was a sliver and the stars blinked down as if in doubt. We picked our way along the footpath, smelling fresh horse and cow droppings. To the left, half a mile away, was the black hulk of the plantation house, and ahead, set back at the edge of the field, was an even deeper blackness that I knew was the brick wall of the old sugar mill.

There were stories about places like this, that in the old days, before the Civil War, all hands had been pressed into twenty-four-hour service during grinding time, and that during those December and January nights, the tired slaves who manned the machine were wont to grow careless with fatigue. But there was always an overseer or overseer's helper standing by the machinery with a sword, to hack off the arm of any slave who, lurching too near the great grinding wheels, allowed his hand or sleeve to be caught. I didn't know if it was true, but it had been repeated so often that now it had taken on the strength of myth.

My mental meanderings were broken by a cough behind me. I turned.

"You okay?" I whispered.

"Yeah. Just my allergies."

I listened for a moment. He was wheezing.

"We can rest," I said.

"No. Let's keep going."

A shape moved under an oak tree and a head turned in our direction.

"Cows," I whispered. "Let's go around. No need to spook 'em."

We made a semicircle, going around the herd lying by the feeding trough.

"Almost there," I breathed.

Blaize didn't answer but when I checked over my shoulder he was still behind me.

The brick wall of the tumbled structure loomed in front of us and I stopped.

"Stay here," I whispered and crept toward the bricks.

Michelle had said it was a place to look, but as I flashed the light inside, against the bare walls reeking of earth-smell, I saw she was wrong. No one had been here for a long time and there was cow manure on the grass. I shined the light in a corner, the inner sanctum where Michelle said she and the little black children had once played, but there were no tin can lids, no cellophane wrappers, not even old newspaper.

"Well?" Blaize asked.

"Nothing here," I said.

He lurched toward me and I heard his breath coming in ragged gasps.

"Are you going to make it?" I asked.

He nodded, grabbing the wall for support.

"It's just I left my inhaler," he said.

"We can go back."

"No." It was almost a shout. "Not until we find out if he's here."

I nodded at the plantation house and then at the outbuildings just south of it.

"Then we'll have to go there," I said.

Another nod while he sucked in air.

"Look, why don't I go scout it out?" I said. "You wait here and I'll whistle if I find anything."

A fierce head shake. "I'm going."

I saw there was no arguing and started forward, toward the big house, wending my way around piles of brick rubble. I heard Blaize stumble behind me, but when I looked he was still upright.

Something bit into my chest and I gave a little cry, then realized it was barbed wire.

"Careful. We'll have to go under."

I held the strands apart for him and then slipped across while he did the same for me.

His wheezes were louder now, like a leaky bellows. Scenarios raced through my mind: Him collapsing, my having to carry him out. And all along we'd assumed his mother was exaggerating his condition.

The big building loomed before us now, exuding decay. What little light there had once been from stars and fingernail moon had been sucked up by the big house as if the latter were a vacuum and I had the sense of standing on the edge of a precipice, overlooking a whirlpool. Even the trees seemed to have been folded into its blackness, their trunks permanently twisted toward the vortex.

I came to the back porch and stopped.

"What?" Blaize wheezed.

"Nothing." I found the steps and tried the lowest one. It gave under my weight but held. Then I tried the next and the next until I was on the porch.

"Come on," I whispered.

Blaize followed, standing beside me in the center of the porch.

"There's nobody here," I said. "I'm going to turn on the flashlight."

The beam lapped along the rotting floorboards, spilled up onto the sagging back door. I gave the door a push, but it was either locked or nailed shut. I went to the downstairs windows and found one that was broken.

"It doesn't look like anybody's been in here for a long time," I whispered.

"They could have used the front door," Blaize said, breathing fast.

"Well, I don't want to go around there. It can be seen from the road." I carefully removed a jagged glass shard from the pane and stepped through. Dust swirled up from the floor and I sneezed.

"Better not come in," I told Blaize. "It's full of dust."

I might as well have saved my breath. He was tying a handkerchief over his face and now he, too, stepped into the dark room. I flashed the light along the floor. Small, furry things ran squeaking out of the way and I shuddered. We were in what had been the dining room, for there was a long table, covered by a cloth. No kitchen; I seemed to remember that in the older plantation houses the kitchen was a separate structure, outside. I went through the doorway, into the living room and gasped when I saw the ghosts. Except they weren't ghosts, just furniture covered by sheets.

I ran the light across the walls. No one had taken down the paintings and I saw that one was of a beautiful young woman with night-black hair and a demure smile. She wore a white bridal gown and I thought she looked almost afraid. But maybe it was my imagination. The spot next to her was a bare square, as if another picture had hung there, but had been removed.

We tiptoed through the rest of the downstairs, the boards creaking under our feet, and at one place the wood gave way and I jumped back.

I went around the rotten spot and scanned the downstairs sitting room. There was an old treadle-type sewing machine and a rocking chair, but nothing to show anyone had been here for years. Unlike the other rooms, this one exuded a faint odor of mothballs.

"What about up there?" Blaize asked, pointing.

I followed his finger and saw the staircase.

"Okay."

I tested the risers with my weight, one by one. They gave but held me. When I reached the top I turned and waited for Blaize. He seemed thinner, his dark eyes larger in the glow of the flashlight, almost as if his atoms were on the verge of flying in all directions.

"I don't think he's up here," I said. "I don't think anybody is. But I guess we've come this far."

I made my way down the hall, past peeling wallpaper, to a room at the end. The master bedroom, I guessed, because it held a canopied four poster bed like I'd seen at my grandmother's house while my mother was still alive. There was a desk, an armoire, and even an enamel chamber pot just under the bed itself. There was a smell in this room that was worse than in any of the others, worse than decay, worse than mere mildew or mold. It was something I'd never smelled before, not even from animal carcasses rotting on the road, and it awakened a sense of dread I couldn't explain. I wheeled and bumped into Blaize in my hurry to get out the door.

"You smelled it, too," he said.

"Yeah."

We went down the hall to the other room, wondering what we would find and not really wanting to know.

I stopped at the closed door.

"You really want to?" I asked Blaize.

He nodded. "We've got to."

I pushed it gently open, surprised that it swung noiselessly on its hinges.

"Damn," I said and stopped, Blaize bumping into me.

"What?"

"Look." I moved the circle of light from the bunk bed in the corner to the wooden toy chest at the bed's foot, to the Lionel train set on the floor. A tiny flagman held his lantern permanently on high and a signal arm showed red, as if by rising it had stopped the train forever.

"Who?" Blaize asked.

Before I could answer we heard the creak from below, echoing up like a shot.

"Oh, Christ," I breathed.

"Rats?" Blaize asked, hopeful.

But he'd barely said it when we heard it again, and I recognized it for what it was: the sound of a door being pushed open on rusted hinges.

We stood paralyzed as the steps made their way slowly across the big living room.

I looked around, frantic. There was a closet but whoever it was would surely look inside.

The steps went into the dining room, halted, then came back. Then, to my horror, I heard the first riser of the stairs squeak.

I eased the door shut and flashed the light on the window over the bunk bed.

"Come on," I whispered, dragging Blaize after me.

I pulled him across the room, knocking the train off the tracks as we went, feeling the tiny cars and figures cracking under our feet. I stood on the bed, flashed the light through the window. There was a tree outside, and, thank God, a limb.

"We've got to climb out," I whispered.

"I . . ." He whispered, his breath crackling.

The intruder was halfway up the steps now, coming slowly, deliberately, as if he knew there was no escape.

I reached down, tugged on the sash, and the window edged upward with a groan.

"Go on," I hissed. "Get on the limb. When you get to the trunk shinny down."

"Colin . . ."

"Now!" I ordered, shoving him forward. He bent over, and grabbed the limb with both hands. Seconds later he was straddling it, pulling himself along with his arms.

The steps were just outside the door now. The handle was turning.

I stuck the flashlight in my belt and ducked through the window. I found the limb, and, legs across it, followed Blaize. He was at the crotch of the tree now, but once there, wasn't moving.

"Come on," I said. "You have to climb down."

"I can't find any limbs."

"Then drop. It isn't that far."

"Colin . . ."

I nudged him but he wouldn't budge.

"I can't," he said.

"The hell you can't," I said, and pushed hard. He lost his grip and I heard him give a little cry as he fell, landing with a thump on the ground below.

I hugged the trunk, then let myself slide downward, skinning my arms on the rough bark as I fell.

I hit the earth and jackknifed backward, onto my side. I rolled over and sat up.

"Are you all right?" I asked.

"I think so," he wheezed, and then broke off into a fit of coughing.

"Come on. We have to get back to the car." I helped him up and we started across the big yard, the high grass brushing our ankles. The cemetery was half a mile away, across open pasture. If we didn't stop we had a chance of making it.

We reached the edge of the front yard and found our way blocked by another fence. I pushed down on the bottom wire to hold it for Blaize but when I turned he was twenty steps behind, wheezing.

"Quick," I said. "Get under."

"I don't . . . think . . . they're coming after us," he choked out.

I waited while he held the wires apart for me and then ducked through.

"Doesn't matter. They will be."

"Maybe we can . . . walk."

"No." The cemetery, impossibly far away, was a smudge of black against the lighter sky. "Come on, I'll help you."

I trotted beside him as he half ran, half walked, his breaths becoming more ragged with each second.

We came to the live oak in the center of the field and stopped.

"I can't go any more without resting," Blaize said.

I looked around. Maybe whoever it had been had lost us, given up. Maybe, nestled in the shadow of the big tree, we were invisible.

The outbuildings were to our right, blocking our view of the River Road, and to our right, between the tumbled sugarhouse and ourselves was what appeared to be a storage shed. But there were no lights, no sounds of movement from any of them.

"Let's go," I said. "It's only another quarter mile."

Blaize lowered his head, though whether it was a nod I couldn't tell.

"Come on." I grabbed his arm and we lurched out into the pasture, away from the comforting cover of the tree.

We'd only gone twenty feet when I heard the ground pounding somewhere to my left. Pounding like someone with a mallet . . .

With a sick feeling I realized they were hoof beats. And they were coming closer.

I glanced over my shoulder, caught a blur of movement near the storage shed. Then it seemed to grow in size until something detached itself, became another form entirely.

A horseman.

"Run!" I yelled. "Now!"

I'd only gone a few steps when I heard Blaize give a little cry and when I turned I saw him on the ground, crouching where he'd fallen, and the horseman was almost at his side, reaching down.

I felt something against my ankle, stopped, picked up a fragment of brick and without aiming threw it as hard as I could.

A grunt of pain came from the horseman and he toppled from the saddle. I rushed back, helped Blaize to his feet, and pulled him forward again.

"Colin . . ." His voice was a bare whisper.

"You can make it," I promised.

Then night turned to day as brightness exploded around us and I felt the world spinning.

CHAPTER NINETEEN

It is time. I put the car into gear and edge back out onto the River Road, careful to avoid a red sports car coming from the other direction, a middle-aged man with sunglasses at the wheel.

Gloria Santana had a red MG, given her by her father when she graduated from college. We'd all noticed and commented on it. I wonder what happened to the MG. Did it sit in her driveway until the tires rotted or did her father finally send someone to haul it away, selling it to someone who never knew who its owner had been?

The car that passes is a Corvette, the man behind the wheel, with his open collar and blowing hair, probably a lawyer or investment executive. I have never owned a sports car, though when I was in high school, I thought it would be the key to make me popular with the opposite sex. But somehow after the death of Gloria Santana, the desire to own a sports car vanished, and for the rest of my life I have driven nondescript vehicles, starting with a used Mercury in college and graduating, successively, to station wagons and vans and now, most recently, a Toyota Roadrunner. None of them has been red.

The Corvette was coming from the direction of Windsong and I wonder if they've rebuilt the old place. Or maybe the man in the Corvette was just out for a ride.

I ease the accelerator up to twenty-five. The levee is emerald green, with a fringe of blue wildflowers at its base, and I know that around the next curve I will see it, and I wonder what I will feel.

But I have only gone a few tenths of a mile before I realize something is wrong.

In the first place, the shotgun cabins that used to line the River Road, stretching from Bergeron's store to the boundaries of the plantation, are gone, and the pasture holds no cattle or horses. The barbed wire fence is gone, too, and in its place is a low brick wall, with artificially patched sections designed to give the impression of age. In the distance, a quarter of a mile from the road, I see houses, shimmering like palaces in the sunlight, steep-roofed structures of brick with wide windows. I hunt for the hulking ruin of the plantation house but there is nothing, just a single line of oaks shading a paved boulevard that leads inward toward a larger building. I stop before brick gate posts with a guardhouse in the middle of the boulevard. The guardhouse has been built to resemble a pigeonnaire, with its steep roof and square configuration, but it is glass on all four sides, and a man in uniform sits inside, manning an electric gate. A faux-antique sign on one of the posts says WINDSONG COMMUNITY AND GOLF COURSE. The guard looks up, waiting to see if I am one of the privileged, like the man in the Corvette, but I keep going. In the distance, over the low wall, are the gently rolling hills of a green, and I see the flags for the holes, and a lake in the center.

Maybe, I tell myself, I have mistaken the place, and the real plantation is still ahead, but just before the curve, where the brick wall ends, I see it, a path leading back to a cluster of cedars. The cemetery.

I pull in and stop, shocked by what should not have been a surprise.

It is all gone, leveled for a golf community. The house that we escaped from that night, the field where we ran, the outbuildings, even the sugar mill ruin. All that is left is the cemetery, but I do not want to go there.

I try to envision that night, but it is difficult, because I see Blaize and myself running across the green, dodging a golf cart with two duffers. Where was it that it happened, near the hole over there? Or was it by the sand trap? I am disoriented, adrift. I have come all this way, fearing what I would see, and now I realize there is nothing. I feel at once relieved and cheated, because now all I have is the memory and how can I be sure it happened at all?

But it did.

• • •

When I awoke I was lying on a hard surface, staring up at wooden rafters. My head throbbed and when I tried to move it the room lurched and the contents of my stomach wanted to spill out through my mouth. I tried to move my arms but they refused to obey. For some reason there was a ringing in my ears.

I knew I was dreaming, because this was the way it always happened in nightmares: The slow-motion run as if you were submerged in water, nothing working, legs barely moving, no part of my body responding to commands from my brain, while something unspeakable gained on me.

Except that this time it had caught me and I was at its mercy.

With a matter-of-factness born of shock it came to me that maybe I was dying. Maybe I had been paralyzed, my spine broken, and soon even the nerve impulses that allowed me to breathe would shut down.

I tried my arms again and this time I felt movement in my fingers. They scratched a rough surface I finally recognized was wool. I was lying on a blanket.

Then I heard Blaize's breathing. It was coming in desperate gasps, from somewhere above and to the right. This time when I willed my head to turn it did and I saw him just above me and to the side, huddled on a bunk.

But where? We weren't in the upstairs room of the plantation house. The walls here were bare, just gray boards, and all I could make out was a chair.

I was shaken out of my thoughts by the voices.

"I told you not to put those things out," a voice said. "I begged you."

It was slightly muffled, coming from somewhere outside the room.

"I told you somebody would get hurt."

"And I told people to stay off the place," another voice answered. This one I recognized: it was Sikes.

"That doesn't mean you can booby-trap the fields. For Christ's sake, they're just kids."

"You were just a kid, too."

"That was a long time ago. It's over."

"Don't tell me it's over. Things like that ain't never over. Kids come around, people get blamed."

"Everybody's forgotten. You can't keep fighting what happened then. My father's dead."

"Your father? You still call Gaston Drood your father? Haven't you learned by now I'm your father? I'm the one stood up to him, I'm the one threatened him, I'm the one protected you after he . . ."

"I know."

"You know what the bastard had the nerve to say to me? He said, 'It's not like he was really my son.' That was his excuse."

"But he's dead."

"Yeah, he's dead, but nobody needs all that raked up. They come around asking questions, running all over the place . . .

I kept this place for you. I stayed here while you was up north. Because I knew some time you'd be back. I knew my son was coming back one day."

I listened thunderstruck. I'd completely misunderstood what Michelle had told us, and she probably hadn't understood either.

After what Drood done to my son somebody ought to kill him . . .

Only it wasn't Darwin Drood who'd molested Sikes' son. Darwin Drood was Sikes' son, and it was Darwin's supposed father, the man who owned Windsong, who'd molested Darwin.

Sikes had fathered Darwin by the old man's wife and she'd either killed herself or been murdered by her angry husband soon after giving birth.

"All these years," Sikes was saying. "All these years. I deserve something."

"But not to set traps for people."

"They wouldn't of stepped on it if they'd of stayed away."

"But don't you see what this means? The law'll come out here. We'll both be charged. We have to let them go."

"That's just why we can't let 'em go, son. The first boy was different. You just give him money, sent him on his way. When he gets tired of running he'll call his folks and they'll come get him, wherever he is. Wasn't nothing done to him. You just saw him hiding on the levee and helped him out. No crime in that. But this is different."

Silence, punctuated by Blaize's wheezing. He wasn't saying anything and I didn't know if he was conscious or not.

"You don't understand," Sikes said again, speaking slowly, as if to a retarded child. "This place, Windsong, is mine. I've worked it all my life. I deserve it. Ain't never had nothing to call my own. I have a right to protect it, to keep people away, to . . ."

"It isn't yours," Darwin Drood said quietly. "It's mine, remember?"

"Legally, yeah. But you're my son, my flesh and blood. If you've got a right, I got a right. You can't deny me that."

"I'm not denying you anything. I've told you that you can stay here as long as you want. But not this way."

I willed myself to roll onto my side. The numbness caused by the explosion was wearing off and the ringing in my ears had receded to a dull buzz.

"Son, what other way is there? They got it in for me in town. Old Bergeron and the rest of 'em would do anything to see me in jail. This is all they need."

"But these are just boys."

"I know, and it sorrows me to have to do it. But I'm trying to protect you and Windsong."

"Don't tell me that!" The younger man was shouting now. "You're just trying to protect yourself!"

"No use arguing," Sikes said. "I'll take care of it. You go on back to the house."

"The house isn't fit to live in. I haven't been in it since it happened fifteen years ago. Until tonight. This is my house. That's why I brought them here, to protect them."

"Then go ride your horse, I don't care. It's best you not see."

I was on my hands and knees now. There was a window just above the bunk where Blaize tossed, unconscious. I had to get out, reach the car, drive for help.

"I won't let you," I heard Darwin shout. It was followed by a thud and a grunt and I realized one man had struck the other. I climbed onto the bed, lifted the sash, and, climbing out the window, dropped onto the ground.

It took a moment for me to get my bearings. Then I realized I was outside one of the buildings to the side of the main house. This must be where Darwin Drood had taken up residence while he mulled over repairing the big house. I tried to get my bearings. Which way was the cemetery?

"Hey, you!"

With a sick feeling I recognized Sikes' voice. His head was peering through the window. I started for the cemetery, then realized I wouldn't make it. My only hope was the River Road and then up the side of the levee, to the batture.

Unless there were other booby traps.

I took off at full speed.

"Come back here, damn you!"

I heard him behind me now, his feet pounding after me. I'd never been fast, but I felt a surge of energy born of adrenaline.

I reached the fence and jammed my foot onto the middle wire, propelling myself half over.

"I said come back here . . ." His hand grabbed my leg and I kicked out, eliciting a curse. I dropped onto the other side, in the berry bushes, feeling the stickers grab my skin and clothes. I fought myself free, ignoring the pain, and beat my way across the gravel, to the levee. I leapt the ditch and pulled myself through the fence, leaving bits of shirt and skin on the barbed wire. I raced up the slope, vaguely aware that Sikes was trying to disentangle himself from the briars.

If I could reach the borrow pit, find the way across to the batture . . .

I turned at the top and looked back. He was at the second fence now, cursing the briars. I fled down the levee, toward the trees at the bottom. I was upriver from our camping spot and I didn't know if there was a place to cross here. I fumbled for the flashlight, shined it in the foliage, but the shadows seemed to mock me. I cut the light and thrust myself into the bushes, feeling thorns grab my skin and clothing. The smell of stagnant water was all around and I fought my way toward it. The pit wasn't deep, not more than three feet. I could wade it and if I made it across he wouldn't be able to follow.

I heard him running down the levee now, toward me, and a

light stabbed out, painting a white circle on the trees twenty feet to my left.

Jesus, he had a flashlight, too.

I froze while the beam moved slowly away from me, then went out.

If I just stayed quiet, like a rabbit huddling in the undergrowth, maybe he wouldn't see me, would give up and leave . . .

His steps thudded on the packed earth of the levee's toe and I realized with horror that he was coming toward me.

Don't move. For God's sake, I can't let myself move . . .

I thought of the saints I'd prayed to in childhood, tried to recall which was the one who helped people in this kind of danger, decided there wasn't any, and gritted my teeth.

All at once the light flared on, blinding me.

"There you are!" he cried and I saw an arm reaching for me. I pulled away but the briars held me like chains and his hand grasped the front of my shirt. I smelled his reeking breath and squirmed to free myself but his grip was like a steel trap.

"I told you kids to stay away," he said, still huffing from the chase. "I told you, didn't I? I said 'Stay off Windsong.' But you wouldn't listen. Wouldn't none of you listen and now look."

He pulled me toward him and I felt the briars giving up their hold.

"I told you and you came anyway and now I gotta do what I gotta do."

"No," I begged but he was dragging me by the arm now, and there was nothing I could do but follow.

"Don't give me no pleasure. I want you to know that. Don't give me no pleasure at all. But I gotta protect what's mine."

"Let me go!" I cried but he only pulled me faster, up the slope.

"You and your friend. You shoulda stayed at home. Damn, but you shoulda stayed at home. Now . . ."

He stumbled on the uneven ground and that was when I jerked away, heading back downhill.

"Hey, goddamn you . . . !" He screamed after me and I heard his steps a few feet behind. "Get your ass back here!"

I leapt into the foliage and this time the briars weren't as thick. I felt my feet sinking into the mud, as the wet earth pulled at my shoes.

I had to make it across the borrow pit.

"You can't get away, damn you! You might as well quit now!" he yelled.

I reached the edge of the water and plunged in, feeling the mud suck at my feet.

Keep going. That was the key to not getting stuck. Keep up the forward motion or the gumbo will suck you down, hold you like the tarbaby . . .

I willed my legs to rise, but the further I went the harder it was. The water was to my knees, now to my waist. I pushed hard with my left leg to propel myself forward and felt my left foot sinking deeper into the mud. Fear iced through me as I realized I was held fast, unable to go forward or back. The light flared on, pinning me in its glare.

"I told you," Sikes said, breathing heavily. "I told you, boy. You didn't have to make it this hard. It coulda been easier, painless. Now look."

I heard one of his hands moving, sensed he was pulling something out of his belt.

"Now I got to go in and make sure you sink."

"Please . . ." I begged.

"I'm sorry, boy. But you got to see: I got no choice."

The light wavered and I caught movement, sensed his pistol being leveled, and tried to throw myself flat on the surface of the water, flailing with my arms like a drowning swimmer, but my legs refused to budge. A whimper of fear escaped from my throat and then the shot exploded the night.

At first I thought the shock of the bullet had left me numb, and when the light dropped away, I sensed he'd seen the effect and was on his way to fish out my dying body. But then I heard a grunt, saw the light rake off at an angle, heard other steps behind him.

A second light jabbed out, touching the trees over my head and then coming down to rest on my immobile body.

"You all right, son?"

I blinked in the glare.

"Who?"

"You don't got to worry," Bergeron's voice said. "Sikes ain't gonna bother nobody else never."

CHAPTER TWENTY

Now I stand on the cemetery road and look up at the levee. With the new golf course, I don't know if I can remember where I crossed the fence that night. I think it was further north, but the fence is newer there, festooned with warning signs. I did not come this far to be deterred by signs and I tell myself that if I walk along the levee, maybe I will be able to find the place.

It is a foolish hope. Blaize is almost certainly right. Everything will have changed. But it is something I have to do.

I walk quickly across the tar surface to the fence, testing the strands with a foot. I am thicker now, sixty-three years old, and I don't know if I can wedge my body between the middle and the top strands without catching my clothes. I put my foot on the middle strand and push down, testing whether it will hold my weight. For a second I sway in the sunlight, knowing that if I don't make the effort it will all have been for nothing. Then I ease my other leg over the top strand and put it down on the middle strand, as well. Now I feel the top strand against my crotch, the barbs biting into my most tender parts. When I try to shift my left leg, bring it over to the other side, my weight bears down on my right foot and the barbs dig deeper into my testicles. I hope no one will pass and witness this slightly ridiculous figure of an aging man caught wavering atop a fence in a place he has no business to be.

Maybe, I think, I will stay up here forever, in a frozen segment of time. Maybe I will not have to come down. Maybe, like a stylite, people will bring me food and drink. Maybe I do not really want to move.

I finally push hard with my left leg, grit my teeth against the biting barbs, and feel the crotch of my trousers give. I grab the wooden post, waver for a moment, and then catch the middle strand with my left foot and lower myself to the ground, sensing a draft between my legs where the cloth has been torn. It is, I tell myself, a small price to pay.

I pick my way up the slope, which seems steeper than I remember, the grass more slippery. I step over cow pods and around crawfish chimneys and finally pause at the top, breathing in the unique smell that I remember. It is redolent with decaying organics and stagnant water but there is another element I had forgotten—the pungent odor of diesel fuel, leaking from barges and ships.

I look up, see a hawk gyring slowly above, and wonder what he sees. Nothing has changed for him, because his life is short. He will not remember beyond the last mouse or rabbit or squirrel, plucked from the underbrush below.

It was upstream, I think, as I walk north along the levee top, in the little clump of trees at the foot of the levee: That is where I ran that night and I strain to make it out. But how can I be sure? It could be the clump a hundred yards north, by the next fence post. The truth is that Blaize was right: it has all changed and I have no idea where it was.

• • •

The case against Dr. Benson Chandler was dropped a week after Sikes' death at the hands of Alcide Bergeron. I only heard about it on TV because my father kept me inside the rest of the summer and I didn't drive again for a year. But from what I gleaned from Toby—who called to ferret out information he could use to build up his credit with the same classmates who scorned him—the case against Chandler had begun to break down even before. Now, with Sikes dead—caught almost in the act of murder, though the local paper, in those days of managed news, was more discreet—the case was closed, because the probable murderer was dead. Stan was found in New Orleans, where he'd gone with money Darwin Drood had provided him. He had not been molested and nothing was done to Drood, who retreated even more into the isolation of his decaying estate. I never saw Stan Chandler again because he was sent to an out-of-state camp and his family moved to Ohio, where I was told his father got a job at a research institute. Blaize survived only because Bergeron, having been alerted by his daughter, had called the sheriff before he set out with his rifle in hand. My father and Blanche St. Martin talked several times on the phone and, though I could not hear what they said, it was clear that the tenor was that our little group should be dissolved. Accordingly, Blaize went to a private Catholic boarding school for the remainder of his high school years and I saw him only once. We had little to say to each other.

I never saw Michelle Bergeron again because I was never again allowed to go near the levee. At first I had resented her fleeing, but later I realized that, had she stayed, her father would never have come to save us.

The solution to the case seemed grudgingly satisfactory, because no one had trouble believing Rufus Sikes was a killer. Gloria Santana had gone to the cemetery to meet someone that night, though who was never known. Toby liked to say it was Mr. Cornwall but that was only his speculation. Everyone else thought it more likely that it was her lover, Dr. Chandler. But Sikes had seen her there and, with his insane need to protect his domain, had stabbed her to death. There was no corroboration of other women killed and I gradually realized that was only hearsay from the folk along the River Road, who were willing to attribute any villainy to the old overseer. But there would always be a lingering doubt as to whether the right man had died. You could see it in peoples' eyes, the tone of their voices, when Dr. Chandler's name was mentioned. What if he really had made it out there that night? What if Sikes had just been a crazy old man but had taken no part in the teacher's murder? What if it had been a member of the Chandler family? Stan's mother or his older brother or even Stan?

Long after the family moved, people sometimes joked that Gloria's spirit inhabited the old Chandler house on LSU Avenue, even though the murder had occurred miles away and she had never been known to set foot on the place.

It is an odd fact that a few months after the death of Sikes Windsong burned to the ground, leaving only its brick columns standing. At first, there was talk of a faulty electrical connection, but then someone said the place hadn't had electricity for years, so it must have been lightning, though there was no storm at the time. But I had my own theory and that was that it was done by its owner, Darwin Drood, who wanted to blot out all the pain it had come to represent for him.

I was told he stayed out there, in the outbuilding he had made his home, but some time after I went away to college in Colorado he disappeared.

Now, a lifetime later, I have faced the demons, but I am still dissatisfied. I had foolishly expected to come back to something that was the way I'd left it, look it in the eye, and tell it I wasn't afraid, and yet everything is changed.

Even Sikes' face, which I cannot remember, because it resembles that of a man I saw die two months ago.

So maybe none of the memories are true.

Or all of them.

I hear my name and turn.

Someone is coming down the levee, toward me, and I wonder if it is a caretaker, come to run me off, except that there is no one who would recognize me after all these years.

Then I see Blaize.

"I saw your car down there," he says, smiling. "I thought you might be here."

"I thought you avoided the levee."

"I did. But seeing you after all this time . . ." He heaves a deep breath. "I didn't ask you to come, Colin. I didn't want you to. But you did. And once you did it all came back."

"I'm sorry."

He shrugs, the same little shrug I remember from the old days.

"It's okay."

I nod at the borrow pit, half-hidden by the trees. "You were right. I couldn't find the place."

"What do you think about the golf course?" he asks. "I didn't tell you about that."

"I wonder if the people there know."

"I doubt it."

I breathe in the moisture-laden air.

"How's the asthma these days?"

"Under control."

"That's good."

"I was thinking about Stan," I tell him. "I wonder if he has bad dreams."

"Doesn't everybody?"

"But to know people were whispering about him, his mom, his father."

"It sucked, as the kids say."

I nod, kick at the ground as if the clump of grass at the toe of my shoe is an obstacle that must be removed.

"I'm sorry I left you that night," I finally manage.

"If you'd stayed Sikes would have killed us both."

"That's what I keep telling myself, but we both know the truth: I ran away."

He stares into the trees. "We all run away from something."

I glance at him from the corner of my eye. There is something off-key about his tone.

"But there's just so far you can go," he continues.

"You didn't run," I say. "You stayed right here."

"I didn't run because my mother wouldn't let me. I was a St. Martin. St. Martins don't run. But I ran, Colin. I ran inside. I ran from me."

"Well, we all do some of that."

"No." His voice is firm, in the way it was so many years ago when he'd insisted we should go find Stan. "You don't understand. That's why I didn't want to see you again. But maybe I was wrong."

"About what?"

"Remember when we used to go around with Toby? Remember all those names he used to call me? How he used to joke about fags and blow jobs and queers."

"I remember." My voice trails off as I glimpse where he is going.

"It was a big deal then," he says. "Proving you were a man. If you couldn't prove you were a man, you were a girl. You had to prove you had balls. To everybody. Your parents, your friends, your teachers, yourself."

"It was a tough time." Even to me my voice sounds weak, unconvincing. "We didn't know much then."

"Nobody did," he says angrily. "There was a lot of pain. You had to be what they expected. You had to live for them."

I wait, knowing better than to interrupt.

"Well, I did for a long time. I did what they wanted. I did what she wanted. What she expected. I'm not sure she ever really wanted me to marry, because that meant leaving her. But she wanted the respectability of everybody's knowing I was like everybody else."

"Blaize, you don't have to explain."

"So I did it. I married the first woman who made herself available and we had a son. He's a fine boy, too. He deserves better. But I just couldn't be what they all wanted. I couldn't be a husband or a son. I had to be what I was." He turns to look me in the eye. "And what I was, was queer."

"Hey, it doesn't matter."

"It took me a long while to realize it. I fought it, I really did. But it was there all along. Even back when I was with you guys I knew I was different. I think Toby knew it, too. That's why he said all those things."

"Toby was full of shit."

Blaize nods. "He was about a lot of things. But not this. On this, he was dead on. He knew it before I did."

"And that's why you didn't want to see me," I say. "Jesus, man, it doesn't matter."

"Sure it matters. You just don't understand why."

"No."

He reaches out then, rests a hand on my shoulder, soft as a caress, then turns.

"Let's go back. I want to take you somewhere."

"What?"

He smiles. "Don't worry, I'm not going to put a move on you."

"Oh, for Christ's sake, Blaize, I didn't think . . ."

"Didn't you? Sorry, maybe I'm too sensitive. Anyhow, I have a friend. We've been together since the year after the divorce."

"I'm glad."

"Yeah. He's HIV but things seem to be under control, at least for now."

We stand for a moment in awkward silence and then he nods at the top of the levee.

"Come on home. I'd like you to meet him. Then there's somewhere else I want to take you."

"Sure."

• • •

Phillip Rowell is a muscular, gray-haired man with sharply-chiseled features and piercing blue eyes. As we sit on the patio drinking lattes he tells me he's a tax attorney with a firm whose name I don't recognize but he is thinking of retiring in a year or two so he and Blaize can travel. When Blaize vanishes into the house, Phillip and I watch the blue jays splash in the birdbath near the wooden fence. He tells me he designed and built the backyard, with its fountain, stone-bordered gravel walk, and flowerbeds. He says the squirrels are a nuisance because they rob the bird feeder but that you could have worse problems.

I like him at once and I guess his mentioning that he likes my books doesn't hurt.

"You know, Blaize has talked about you a lot," he says.

"Really? I thought that was a part of his life he wanted to forget."

"There are things you can try to forget but you never can. Besides, I think you were one of the bright parts of that time."

"He may not feel that way since I came back."

Phillip smiles and fingers the handle of his cup.

"Your call was a surprise, of course. But I'm not sure that afterwards he didn't decide it was something God had arranged to bring everything to an end and close the book. He's lived with it for a long time, just like you have. When he told me what you'd told him on the phone, I told him he couldn't put it aside any more."

Blaize reappears then, holding a pair of pants.

"I think these will fit," he says, handing them to me. "I hope you don't mind, Phillip. You haven't worn them for years and you and Colin are about the same size. Colin can't go off in pants that have a hole in the crotch."

Phillip chuckles. "We wouldn't want that."

"You can change inside," Blaize says.

I don't question, just take the pants, head into the living room and change while the two companions sit on the patio, talking. When I am done I rejoin them.

"See?" Colin says. "Perfect." He rises.

"I'll be back in a while," he tells the other man, who nods.

Blaize turns to me. "Do you know where Victorian Manor is?"

"No."

"You can follow me, then. It's just a couple of miles."

• • •

I follow him to a busy boulevard and turn left. Half a mile further, at a blinking traffic signal, we go left again, this time onto the grounds of what looks like a series of condos. There are palm trees and lawns that resemble Astroturf, and a sign that says VICTORIAN MANOR ASSISTED LIVING CONDOMINIUMS.

We creep down the boulevard, passing over three speed bumps, and slide into parking places in front of the main building.

When I get out Blaize waits in front of the big glass doors and explains:

"My mother's ninety-three. She may not recognize you. Sometimes she doesn't even recognize me. But I wanted you to see her before you left. Little things mean a lot to her."

We enter a lobby smelling of vanilla air freshener and Blaize talks to a woman at a desk and she smiles. Then we head right, down a hallway, past an old man in a kimono, who leans heavily on a walker while his colostomy bag dangles from an aluminum rod.

"It can be pretty depressing," Blaize whispers. "That's why I hate coming sometimes. But I try to make it a couple of times a week."

Blaize, always the dutiful son . . .

We come to a closed door and he takes a deep breath.

"Let me go in first," he says. "Make sure she's in a condition to see people."

I nod while he opens the door and then closes it behind him.

I think of the execution chamber and shudder. Executions are over quickly, but here people linger until they degenerate into a vegetative state. I don't want to be here, but there is no graceful way to refuse. And, besides, I sense Blaize has some reason.

The door opens again.

"You can come in now," he announces, his voice slightly off-key.

I walk into the room. There is a bed, a television that is off, and a middle-aged woman in white, standing beside a window that frames a vast field with trees and a lake. So still is the figure in the wheelchair, facing the window, that at first I don't see her at all. Then Blaize walks over to the window.

"Mother," he says. "You have a visitor."

The old head shifts slightly and I walk over to the window so she can see me.

"Mrs. St. Martin," I say. "Do you remember me? Colin Douglas?"

It takes a while for me to see in the withered features a semblance of the face I hold in memory. The hair is white and the skin is a net of wrinkles but the eyes are the same and when she

looks up there is no mistaking. She is dressed like a store mani-
kin, in a suit that I know I saw on her forty years ago, and her
skeletal body is bedecked with jewelry, as if at any moment she
expects the Queen to enter the room so that she will have to rise
from the wheelchair and curtsy.

She reaches out a fragile hand and I take it, careful not to
crush the brittle fingers.

"Why, Colin, it was so nice of you to come. Where are you
now?"

"Colorado, just outside Boulder."

"Colorado. Imagine that. Are you married?"

I tell her about my family and she beams, still holding my
hand.

"That's wonderful. You know, Blaize has a son."

"He told me."

"He comes to visit sometimes."

"I'm glad."

"What do you do these days?"

"I write books."

"Imagine. What kind of books?"

I try to laugh it off. "True crime. Bloody stuff."

Her brows arch. "You surprise me. I always worried when
Blaize was with those other boys but never when he was with you.
You were always such a good boy. And how is your father?"

"He passed away some time ago."

She frowns. "I wonder why I didn't hear? I'm so sorry." She
squeezes my hand, the pressure little more than a twitch of her
fingers. "He was a fine man. I knew your mother, too. I knew
her family."

"Yes, ma'am."

"And that other boy, what was his name? Stanley? Where is
he now?"

"I don't know."

"He was such a polite child. But there was something about his family . . . I can't remember what it was, something that happened . . ." She turns her face up to her son. "What was it about them, Blaize?"

"It wasn't anything, Mother."

"Oh." She slips her hand from mine. "I get confused sometimes. I have trouble remembering some things."

"It's all right, Mother," Blaize says.

"Blaize is so fragile." Blanche St. Martin looks up at me. "You will be careful with him, won't you? You won't stay out in the night air? It's his asthma, you know. His health is delicate . . ."

But I've long since stopped hearing her because I am frozen in place, staring at the old woman, staring at her powdered face, the garish red lips, the gold necklace with the little sapphire pendant, staring at the diamonds and emeralds on her fingers, staring at the gold earrings with dangling five pointed stars . . .

Staring until all the sounds of their talking recede to a low buzz and I feel Blaize's hand on my arm, moving me out of the room and into the light of day.

CHAPTER TWENTY-ONE

"I'm sorry," he says as we stand there on the sidewalk. "I guess it was cowardly of me. Phillip said I should just tell you. I said I couldn't. Then I decided I'd just take my chances, see if you noticed. See if it was meant to be."

"The earrings . . ."

"I lied when I told you I threw that earring away. I took it home and hid it because I knew as soon as you showed it to me it was hers. I was scared somebody would find it. I thought so long as I knew where it was hidden nobody would ever find it. I took the other one and the little box they were in and buried them in the backyard, and when we moved years later I dug it up and took it with me." He rubs a hand across his face, as if testing that this is real and not a dream. "I brought them with me just now. I didn't know until I went into the room whether I'd have the nerve to put them on her. I guess I surprised myself after all."

"I don't understand."

"Sure you do, Colin."

"But your mother . . . why?"

"Think back, Colin. Try to remember how I was back then. Skinny, unsure of myself, kids like Toby making fun of me, calling me queer, and me not even knowing they were right . . ." He smiles sadly. "She felt sorry for me. She thought she could make me something I wasn't. Call it whatever you want. Child molesting, exploitation, or maybe just an act of charity. It ended up getting her killed."

And suddenly I do understand and it is like I am back there again, only now I'm seeing everything in different colors, with different proportions, as if my glasses have been yanked away and the crazy images in front of me are real.

"Gloria," I breathe.

He nods.

"That's right. She thought she could teach me about life. Initiate me. She saw what the others were doing and she felt bad for me. She offered to tutor me and I went to study at her house. Only that isn't all we did."

"Jesus. I never thought . . ."

"I wanted to tell you. I felt badly about it, but I didn't know what to do. I mean, isn't it what all the guys were talking about all the time? What they did with girls? Or what they wanted to do with girls, because back then it was mostly talk. And yet here I was, the ugliest kid in the class and I was doing things they only talked about with a woman ten years older than I was, and she was telling me I wasn't ugly, I wasn't skinny, that everything would be all right."

"How long did it go on?" I ask.

"A couple of months. Until my mother found out."

"How?"

He shakes his head. "Sometimes I used to think she had a sixth sense. Really it was just that she focused on me so hard she could tell when I started acting differently. She pried, she questioned, she even checked my underwear, and I'm sure she followed and watched, because once, when Gloria was supposed to bring me home I thought I saw our car parked in the next block. Once Gloria sent me a note. Just once, and I left it in my top drawer overnight before I burned it. But I had the impression it had been moved. Opened and then refolded and put in a slightly different place. I think that's how she finally got proof."

Blanche St. Martin, the domineering mother, the woman who couldn't bake cookies without burning them, but could hover over her only son like a harpie.

"I felt like hell holding it back from you and Stan," he says. "But how do you admit to something like that? I hated it and yet at the same time I enjoyed it, the physical part. It's not that I can't enjoy sex with a woman."

I nod, not knowing what else to do.

"It's more an emotional thing. I mean, with my wife, it was all right. For the little time it lasted. But it was like we were never really, well, meshing."

"You don't have to explain anything to me."

"But I do, Colin. You're the only one who's left. I can't explain to Stan. It's too late. I don't know where he is and even if I did, his father's probably dead and what could I change?"

"You did the best you could."

"Did I? That's what I've told myself all these years. But I keep thinking about Stan and what he went through. Did he think his father did it finally? Sure, they dropped the charges, but wouldn't there have always been that doubt? Isn't that human nature? How would it have been living like that? Wondering if his father really did do it? Or maybe his mother or his brother?"

I remember my own father, whispering on the telephone from his office, and then going to see Stan's mother. I remember him staying up late the night before, the worried look on his face and all at once I understand, because I've had doubts, too, all these years, and now, too late, they are gone.

"Your mother went to her house."

He nods again. "That's what I figure. She caught her late at night, when Gloria was getting ready for bed. You see, that explains why the cops didn't follow up on the earring: Gloria was getting ready for bed and hadn't been wearing any. If she had, there'd still have been one earring on her when she was found. They probably just figured some coed out screwing with her date dropped it in the bushes, so they didn't check any further."

But my father had seen the earrings before, he just couldn't remember where and on whom, and it never occurred to him that Blanche St. Martin could have been the killer. So he'd gone to the most likely person, Mrs. Chandler, to see if she reacted when he mentioned my finding it.

"I'm sure she took Gloria by surprise. Gloria would have recognized her, let her in, because she was the mother of a student. Then my mother hit her in the head or drugged her. I'm not sure just how because I never asked her."

And wrestled her into the yellow Olds . . .

"She drove out to the cemetery. She probably didn't know you and Stan were camped there that night. But she'd heard me talk about the place and knew it was a lonely location. She pulled Gloria out, but Gloria broke loose."

His voice cracks and his hands start to tremble. I put a hand on his shoulder.

"It's okay. You don't have to say any more."

Because I can see now how it happened, the panicked Gloria fleeing into the forest of tombstones, being caught, the knife rising and falling, the blood spurting, Gloria reaching out in desperation, grabbing for her attacker and managing to wrench off an earring, the knife stabbing down again, the dying woman flinging out her hand, the earring sailing away into the briars . . .

"It must have been about the only time she didn't take a sleeping pill," Blaize says.

And the car Stan and I had seen, the one I thought was white and he thought was a light brown, had really been pale yellow, easily mistaken in the dark . . .

"Oh, Jesus," I blurt.

"What?"

"Michelle." Then I start to laugh and try to stop, embarrassed by the inappropriateness of it, and yet I don't know how to quit.

"Colin?"

"I'm sorry. It's just that now I understand. It wasn't us, it was the car."

"What about the car?"

"When we met Michelle at the cemetery and she ran away. All these years I thought it was because she suddenly had second thoughts, was chicken."

"And?"

"She'd been willing up to then. It was like she'd seen something but she'd seen you and she'd seen me, in the light of day, so what could have scared her? And now I know what it had to be: the car."

"You mean . . ."

"I mean I'll bet she was up that night, too. I'll bet she was waiting for some guy to sneak her out. I'll bet she saw the car go past in a hurry, after Gloria was killed. But being Michelle, she didn't say anything. It wasn't until she saw us pull up that night and saw the same car again that she panicked. Maybe she figured one of us did it after all."

"I never thought about that. But if she hadn't . . ."

"Yeah."

"I wish I knew where Stan was now." He starts toward his car, then stops. "No, I don't. How do you explain about ruining somebody's life?"

"You didn't kill anybody."

"Not physically. But it happened because of me. Because I let it happen."

"You were fifteen, for God's sake."

"Yeah."

"Besides, the only proof is the earring. That wouldn't work in a court of law."

"No. That's what Phillip keeps saying. But we're not talking about a court of law. We're talking about my mother, Blanche St. Martin, and I know what she's capable of. Or what she was capable of then."

"So you protected your mother," I say. "Nobody could blame you for that."

"Nobody but me."

He opens his car door, then turns back to me.

"So there you've got it, Colin. You can do whatever you want with it now. It would make a pretty good book, I guess: *Nympho Teacher Killed by Overbearing Mother Protecting Sissy Son, Who Turns Out Gay Anyway.*"

"I don't plan to write anything," I tell him.

"I'm glad. Not that they could do anything to her now."

"I still wouldn't. It's over. I just had to assure myself that it had happened. I had to be sure of the memories."

"Well, you can be sure now."

"Yeah." I stick out my hand.

"You want to come back to the house?"

"Thanks but I think I still have time to catch a late flight home."

"Good luck, then."

"You, too, buddy." I hold his hand in my grip for a long time, knowing we will probably never meet again, and then, as if by mutual consent, I release it and watch him drive away.

• • •

Back at the hotel I call Colorado. Carolyn answers on the first ring.

"I'm done here," I tell her. "I'm going to put some flowers on my parents' graves and then I'm coming home."

"Everything came out okay?"

I think of the old woman in the rest home, whose mind fades in and out of the present.

"It came out okay."

"I love you," she says and it sounds better than it ever has before.

Three hours later I am looking out of the airplane window as we make a slow circle over the northern part of the city and then nose west. Ten thousand feet below I can see the gleaming silver ribbon of the river, bordered on each side by the green willows that stud the batture.

I am still looking down when a white layer of cloud intervenes, blotting the levee from view.